PIERRE FURLAN is the author of five books of fiction and a number of short literary essays. He is also a leading literary translator, of Paul Auster, Russell Banks, Thomas Savage, Alan Duff and Elizabeth Knox, amongst many others. (He won the 2006 Laure Bataillon prize for the best translation of a work of fiction into French.) He was the French writer in residence at the Randell Cottage in Wellington in 2004-2005, and was literary advisor to the Belles-Etrangères tour of France by twelve New Zealand writers in November 2006. Born in southwestern France, Pierre Furlan spent his adolescence in California and studied at UC Berkeley before settling permanently in Paris, where he is currently working on a novel inspired by his trips to New Zealand.

BLUE~ BEARD'S WORK~ SHOP & OTHER STORIES PIERRE FURLAN

TRANSLATED FROM THE FRENCH BY JEAN ANDERSON

VICTORIA UNIVERSITY PRESS

VICTORIA UNIVERSITY PRESS
Victoria University of Wellington
PO Box 600 Wellington
vuw.ac.nz/vup

Originally published (without 'My Boxing Career', 'Night Shift' and
'Paekakariki') in French by Actes Sud as *L'Atelier de Barbe-Bleue*
L'Atelier de Barbe-Bleue, Pierre Furlan © Actes Sud, 2002
Translation copyright © Jean Anderson 2007
First published 2007

National Library of New Zealand Cataloguing-in-Publication Data

Furlan, Pierre.
L'atelier de Barbe-Bleue
Bluebeard's workshop : and other stories / Pierre Furlan ;
translated by Jean Anderson.
ISBN 978-0-86473-554-6
I. Anderson, Jean. ll. Furlan, Pierre. L'atelier de Barbe-Bleue.
lll. Title.
843.914—dc 22

Ouvrage publié avec le soutien du Centre national du livre—Ministère
français chargé de la culture / Published with the assistance of a grant
from the Centre national du livre of the French Ministry of Culture

Translated with the assistance of a grant from the School of Asian and
European Languages and Cultures, Victoria University of Wellington

Printed by Astra Print, Wellington

Because absence of love is a sin we all know, none of us will remember. That's what we'll call happiness.

CHRISTA WOLF

CONTENTS

MOVING PICTURES

Do you remember, Gaëlle, how we used to say love laughs at barriers, it throws up great invisible bridges and soars over them undaunted, braving fire and ice, then leaps ahead to the next challenge? That day, our last day, it felt as if the heat had left us and gone outside. I knew that if I left too you wouldn't send the great Diahkité or any other witch doctor after me, though you'd threatened to so often. Remember? Professor Mahmoud Diahkité, Stairwell B on the far side of the courtyard, second floor, room 129, expert in bringing straying lovers to heel — *your partner he will come back he will be running behind of you like the dog behind of his master.*

The sun was beating down on the walls, and even squinting we still felt dazzled. 'Look at these desert sands,' you said to me. On Boulevard Raspail, the black roadway shimmered like a lake. Mirages already. And you with your limp, I-dunno smile, your never-knowing smile, you started by mimicking my accent, and when I showed you the grass in my pocket you pouted sweetly and whispered, 'Don't go to any trouble, not here, not now.' But what was wrong with here and now? For once we had a here and now, that heat-stilled afternoon, even the cars were at a standstill, crushed under the layers of melted sky on their bonnets. Not here, not now, that's why we were always nowhere. 'I keeped the best for you,' I said. And you, shaking your head, 'We don't say keeped!' And then me, 'Oh yeah?' It always made me laugh when you turned into the guardian of this formal French garden, such a valiant nation always trimming away any unwanted shoots, chopping the tops off the apple trees, torturing the pear trees, putting down concrete, sand, always suspicious of anything growing untrained. But you were right, it wasn't a time to be smoking, thirty-six degrees in the shade and our faces melting down into our collars. You said, 'Let's go to Rue Récamier, we can sit and watch movies all afternoon. I've got a pass, we won't have to pay.' Inside there was an exhibition, people walking round in silence, bowing low to the paintings and to some guy in glasses talking nineteen to the dozen at the top of his voice and pointing. We didn't even bother to look at these jerks, we went upstairs into the darkened room with the two video screens showing the same images and the tiny speakers crackling away non-stop. We could finally breathe, it was cool – after a bit you put on a little jumper, I wondered where you pulled that out from, unless you'd planned every last detail of the afternoon, and I felt a bit stupid, a bit thick, as you so kindly used to call me.

While the first film was on, I mostly looked at the checked shirt lying across your knees. And your profile. When you opened your mouth it made a lighter spot and I would've liked to put my finger on it, or my tongue. You could feel I was watching you and you'd turn your head and we'd both smile. But the film, whoa, it was totally boring. It went on about art and painting and poetry, but it was like some kind of church with fat guys, bald guys, old wrinklies preaching for some other guy, a poet who'd gone up to heaven and left messages for them.

The second film, that one was about artists in Montparnasse ages ago, I got the impression it was mostly about foreigners, but no Africans. Some guy who babbled on and on kept saying 'negro art' whenever the statues had big lips. It nearly cracked me up laughing but I sat tight because I respect your prophets. What really grabbed me in the film was the way people talked, all rapid-fire volleys like automatic rifles, in breathy high voices – no wonder the speakers were crackling. And it reminded me of old war movies where families cluster around those enormous old radios they used to have, and whenever they look up it's with sort of lit-up faces, like they've been washed clean by the spluttering coming out of the speaker.

While the second film is running, I take your hand, Gaëlle, and you let me hold it for a bit. I can feel the skin of your arm, cold, taut, and the muscles underneath, they're full of electric energy, I wonder where that's coming from. On the screen they're talking about a painter, it's like they're really sucking up to him. There's an old guy, totally wrinkly, it's unbelievable, his whole face, even his forehead and cheeks, it's like he's got mouths all over his face, maybe he got that way from yakking so much because one thing's for sure, he doesn't know how to shut up. He's got one arm missing, too, and his jacket sleeve is waving about like an oar without a rower. It must be cold where they are, I can tell from their coats. The one-armed guy is wearing a hat and there's a cigarette marking the spot where his real mouth is. He's saying that the other guy, the dead artist, was handsome. He even says 'divinely handsome' and in the end it gets to me. Not God again, I think to myself, not again, and I gave you a little nudge with my elbow, Gaëlle. But you didn't react, you were caught up in the film, and when they started to show some of the artist's paintings I saw tears running down your cheeks. The light from the screen was shining on them, the colours were reflected, and that was beautiful as well. I was moved by you, you were moved by the film, and the guys on the screen were moved by themselves. Because the artist, you could tell he was like them, the way they wished they could be, like they would want people to talk about them some day. First they call him a drunk, a drug addict, riddled with TB, and then they say he was poor and violent. But it makes them smile, they shrug their shoulders and end up swearing he's a genius, he's *divine*. His brushstroke never faltered, one of them warbles. At the end they show his nudes. The gorgeous chicks he managed to get hold of, this drunken addict, poor guy, etc. It must've been a lot different in those days. And the most unbelievable bit is his wife. She's just spectacular in the portraits. There's even a statue of her, round and solid, you want to take her in your arms, lay her down and make love to her, and obviously you can't. At that point I look at you, Gaëlle, and the tears are gone. You've slumped down a bit in your seat and to me you look as round as the statue. I think a guy who had a wife like that – even if the portraits and stuff, they're not completely true to life – couldn't have been a total waste of space. And I'd like to take you by the arm, Gaëlle, and show you that we could be like them, but this time you pull your hand away. You're crying again, shiny tracks sketched down your face like scars, is that what's hurting you? The tears cutting your cheeks and drawing blood? No, of course it's the film again, they're saying that those two, the painter and his wife, they loved each other so much that when she heard he'd died from too much alcohol or drugs, she jumped from five floors up and killed herself for ever. Even though she was expecting. Yeah, sure it's sad, Gaëlle, but it happens all the time. Look at Ahmed and Stef and their overdose. There wasn't much of a fuss about that, maybe because most of the art Ahmed left behind was the figures he'd put on the slate, but who cried then? I'm not all that much in favour of making films about it, you know.

So it's the end of the second film, but you don't

want to leave. We're nice and cool now, I say, but you shake your head. Seems to me you want to cry, that's what you came here for. And I have to say it's starting to really piss me off. I could give you a few reasons to cry, ones that'd be more fun for me. But you're not interested in my reasons. And when I said that, you waved your hand like you were chasing away a fly and said that I didn't understand a thing about it, that you were into art, not crying. Fine if some bunch of old guys want to get themselves all excited over seeing de Gaulle shaking hands with Churchill or Gandhi half-naked. Let 'em get their rocks off when they can. But we're young, Gaëlle, it's not right for these old guys to be alive up there on the screen when we're sitting here rotting like a sack of old guts. In the end I said, 'Shit, you know where you can find me tonight if you want me.'

'Yeah yeah,' you muttered.

I'm sorry I haven't seen you again since, but I'm not sorry I left.

I dived down into the Metro with the heat at my heels. In the train, people were sweating, breathing in little gasps like dogs that have run too far. There were two girls standing near the door holding pretty fans. It looked sort of fun, so I went over to them. But when I turned around there was a guy lying collapsed on the floor with one foot up on the seat and one arm hanging out into the aisle. He still had his baseball cap on. A young black guy in shorts and a T-shirt, nothing like a homeless person. Not moving at all and with his eyes turned up in his head. I watched a half-crushed beer can rolling around and banging into the metal wall from time to time. Its clanging was out of synch, like a broken bell – a really annoying racket. Do you think that's why everyone was looking the other way? I don't. Shit, I thought, he must have OD-ed or something, anyway I didn't want him to be dead. On the seat beside this collapsed guy there was an old couple, him with white hair and a navy-blue blazer, reading a newspaper, her all hunched up and with a vague look on her face. The two girls carried on cackling and telling each other stories. At the next stop a third girl got on and made a dive towards the seats. But as soon as she got an eyeful she turned smartly and sat on one of the pull-down seats facing the other way, then started to dust off her white sneakers. The funny thing is, the guy lying there, well, his hand had moved because of the vibrations and it had fallen right next to the girl's butt. She was all busy with her shoes and didn't notice. It was a smooth-skinned hand attached to a well-muscled arm. It could have been the guy in the film, the 'divinely handsome' one, except he was black.

I'm criticising the other passengers, but I was just like them, I didn't really want to know what was going on behind me. I was thinking there'll be a conductor at the last stop. We went on like that as far as Pasteur, I'd just about forgotten the guy on the floor, I was starting to feel better about myself and thinking that the girls with the fans were pretty cool, we're not perfect, that's all. You go your way, I'll go mine, like the song says. At Pasteur, as I was going to get off, this woman appeared. She must have come out of nowhere, because a second before there was just the grey floor, the white sneakers, the newspaper, the smiling fans and the quiet of the train travelling on. This woman from nowhere shouted out, 'For God's sakes, he's not a dog you know!'

She pulled the alarm.

She was a blonde, a real blonde in spite of her dye job, a fat woman in her fifties, as pink skinned as a baby pig, wearing earrings and a practically see-through summer dress. She had an accent, Polish maybe. She got out onto the platform – the train couldn't leave now, you could hear the alarm still shrilling – and I went out calmly to stand with her, as detached as if I'd come from another carriage where nobody knew a thing about any of this.

'He's not a dog, you know, he's a human being!' she said again, looking furiously at me. 'Oh that's true,' I said, 'that's so true.' And hearing it made me feel good, as if she was reassuring me that I was a human being too. But she wasn't even talking to me, she was talking to the Metro worker, a black guy who wasn't in such a great hurry to get there because he didn't really want to see the little surprise waiting for him. The Polish woman was waving her arms around like a windmill and shouting, 'Over here, over here!'

Inside the carriage, the guy with white hair folded up his newspaper, waiting patiently for things to be sorted out.

'And nobody did a thing!' squealed the Polish woman, poking her head into the carriage. You could tell she was trying to work up her courage so she could tell herself that she was in the right in spite of all these bloody idiots who never make a move, who just sit there inspecting their trousers for stains.

Since the old guy didn't respond – the woman who'd been sitting across from him had mysteriously disappeared – the fat Pole went even pinker and shouted at him, 'The day it happens to you, no one will lift a finger to help you either!'

He got up. As he passed in front of us – he was just moving to another carriage to be left in peace – we saw the little ribbon of the Legion of Honour in the lapel of his blazer.

The Metro guy came into the carriage, looking sulky. He walked round the body, thought for a moment, leaned down, stood up again. 'Pfff,' he hissed, 'I don't touch this one without no gloves!'

The Polish woman was now addressing the whole platform, 'He's not a dog, you know, he's a human being.' Then suddenly, reaching a decision, she shot off towards the exit. I fell into position in her wake like a second member of her expeditionary party. I paused for a moment at the foot of the stairs, where a young guy in sandals with a newspaper under his arm, who'd been watching the show, nodded in the direction of the fat blonde. She was climbing the stairs, struggling but determined, wavering from left to right as she went like some strange beast.

He smiled and said, 'You get your fun where you can.'

And off he went, pleased with his witty comment, unaware that the stench trailing behind him was simply his life.

And me, I blamed it all on you, Gaëlle. I tell myself that if you'd been there I would've helped the guy on the floor just to impress you. I'd even have pulled the alarm. That's why I miss you, Gaëlle, because with you I wanted to be better than I am. Instead, sitting here now in the sun bored shitless, I just think. I tell myself things, for example, that the life of the young black guy in the Metro was worth just as much as anyone else's – including Pasteur's, since we were at his station – because what you see everywhere, trying out different bodies, is a single life force, the same one. And if I do nothing for him, dying from an overdose or whatever, I'll do nothing for you, or even for me.

All I'll be doing is talking in the sun. About you, about what you could've done for me when you loved me, Gaëlle.

BLUEBEARD'S WORKSHOP

It was Bluebeard who woke us up, come from afar, down the centuries and the dusty highways and byways while Anne, sister Anne, was transformed into a little woman with long hair who put so much effort into projecting her voice when she spoke that I could see a blue vein swelling up and pulsing on her throat. Ghislaine, our Writer. For the last two days here in this imitation eighteenth-century castle, she'd been leading the creative writing workshop I'd enrolled in for lack of anything better to do. The weather was unusually hot for Belgium, even for July; looking at the photos on the front page of the evening paper, I envied the people on their sunburnt lawns spraying themselves with water from their garden hoses. The workshop was drowsing along on this Wednesday afternoon. And as we went sailing off into our dreams, Ghislaine warned us about particular monsters to avoid, for example the verb 'get' (too flat), using too many adjectives and adverbs (too flowery), and writing run-on sentences (too clumsy). While I found this silly advice amusing, my neighbour Arnaud, a young teacher from Lille, would sometimes start, as if he'd just been struck by a nightmarish thought or a great revelation. When this happened he would hit his forehead with his ballpoint pen to pop out the writing tip, then throw himself at his blank page, his tongue hanging out. I think Ghislaine rather enjoyed this, maybe she found it erotic, but the young woman on the other side of Arnaud, the one he'd been trying to get off with since day one (Elodie Billot, she was in Room 22, and this morning Arnaud had hung his key on the hook for Room 22 and had breakfast with Elodie, as if . . .), smiled at his antics and cast amused looks in my direction that I avoided reacting to. I especially didn't want to move so I wouldn't have to feel the sweat in my socks. Abruptly, in her little piping voice, Ghislaine announced that she was going to tell us the key to success. She was so sure of herself that she added, 'No extra charge. The Key.'

There was an expectant silence, some throat clearing and foot shuffling.

'This story has sold three million copies . . .' Ghislaine began.

'It's about Mary, a young woman from New York, but not too young, divorced, with children at primary school. She works in a gallery, and there's going to be an exhibition of work by a painter from Wisconsin, not very well known but very talented. Jim is tall, dark and handsome, apparently filthy rich and young as well.

All this would be of no consequence, of course, if he weren't interested in Mary, but fortunately as soon as they set eyes on each other it's like an electric current passing between them, love at first sight so strong that, as the author puts it, "her fortress was breached". An intimate dinner. He jumps her, but to show her that it's not just a one-night stand and that he's got plenty of money (remember this is America, where goodness and beauty always go hand in hand), he sends a limousine to collect Mary's children and take them to school the next morning. She goes to work at the gallery "walking on air".

'A week later, Jim asks Mary to marry him. Feeling a bit out of her depth, she asks her next-door neighbour for advice. She tells Mary: "True enough, he has the most gorgeous blue eyes, but I've seen a nasty glint in them." Mary can tell at once that her neighbour is jealous, and she marries Jim. They go off to Wisconsin, to a superb ranch where the children are going to just love the horses.

'Things turn sour pretty much straight away. Jim becomes wildly jealous. He shuts himself away all day in a studio workshop that Mary is forbidden to go into, and he refuses to take down from their bedroom wall the portrait of his previous wife, who died in mysterious circumstances – which puts a bit of a damper on their love-making. When autumn arrives, Jim sends the children off to boarding school and Mary is now forbidden to go anywhere by herself.

'Depressed, worried sick, she finally realises that

Jim's former wife committed suicide and the same thing will happen to her if she stays.

'One day, when Jim is away, she sneaks a key and goes into the forbidden workshop. There she discovers pictures of mutilated women, disembowelled or with their throats slashed; one of them is clearly his ex-wife. This is so horrifying that Mary would faint if she weren't acutely aware that being caught here would be the end of her. She locks the door and runs off unsteadily into the surrounding fields. But someone gives her away. And when Jim gets back that night, he walks straight up to her, demanding to know where she's been. She lies, stammering, while he just stands there in front of her, livid with fury, sniffing at the air: he smells betrayal and, underneath, the tender flesh that he'll be devouring as the price of her betrayal. Mary, shaking uncontrollably, begins to speak, incoherently. "I knew you were crazy," announces Jim the ogre. "If you've lied to me, you'll never see your children again." And with that he rushes off towards his workshop.

'Mary drags herself to her car. She drives off, but when she gets to the boundary of the property she finds the way blocked. "I have to stop you and report to Mr Jim," the guard tells her. She now realises that she's going to end up in the lake. Who will save her?

'The vet! Yes, of course, the new vet, a naïve young man who just happens to be there when she turns back towards the big house. He's come to treat two cows. Emerging from the stable, he comes across a haggard-looking Mary, who grabs him by the arm. "I don't want to die like his first wife," she whispers. In a flash, the vet grasps the horror of the situation, hides Mary in his station wagon under a blanket that smells of cattle, and drives away from the vast property without further ado. "I'm putting my future on the line for you," he declares, blithely heroic. She's afraid he may take her to the psychiatric clinic. She knows that the psychiatrist is entirely on Jim's side, just like the sheriff, who wouldn't get re-elected without Jim's support. But she's wrong. The vet, moved by her pleading, agrees to drive her to the airport at Madison, where she catches a plane for New York. Once there, she hides out at her ex-husband's; after covering her in sloppy kisses, he helps her find a lawyer and inform the police. So the family is reunited, and that's how it ends.'

'Goodness me,' we said, dreamily.

Arnaud whacked himself in the forehead again with his ballpoint and Elodie exclaimed, 'All that just to go back to her husband? Total waste of time.'

'Three million copies,' Ghislaine repeated.

'People are so damn stupid,' concluded one enlightened soul.

Something was stirring within us, something we couldn't put a name to, something that found the 'three million' exasperating. Then Ghislaine added: 'I just wanted to explain to you how you put together a best-seller. You take a well-known story – in this case, Bluebeard – and you update it. People's subconscious hasn't changed over the last five centuries, really.'

'So it's always the same old story?' exclaimed Elodie.

'And here I've been trying to think up something new!'

And that's when I realised I had a chance. Because there's something else that hasn't changed over the centuries, and that's desire. Hormone-fuelled desire. Mine had been working away pretty well since Ghislaine had done her magazine number for us. I thought to myself, 'If I can get her on her own in a dark corner, I'll make her sing a different tune: none of this blathering on about writing, I'll soon have her twittering away like a little bird.'

This was the subject of my next writing exercise. I used the bragging stories of one of my cousins, a sports-mad guy who'd told me all about his philosophy of love one evening in the Café de Cluny. He was furious because his sister-in-law looked down her nose at him, didn't cook up any special little treats when he invited himself around to her place. 'Whose fault is that?' I asked him. 'My brother's,' he shot back at me. 'Because he doesn't know how to handle her. There's a way of screwing women that takes the wind right out of their sails. But you have to really give it to them. Really give it to them! After that, you can hand them your dirty laundry. They won't just wash it, they'll iron it – with love – as well.' This from a guy who was clenching his teeth and his fists as he spoke. And I remember he insisted on paying for our two coffees with a cheque, much to the waiter's annoyance. He liked rugby and foie gras, and he died young – but that's another story.

When I read out my page in front of my fellow

students, and felt something like a chill of disapproval blowing through the room, I knew I was on the right track. Ghislaine looked wide awake. I didn't find her beautiful, but I did want to screw her. Especially since she'd told us her Bluebeard story.

Towards six o'clock, we put away our papers and went out into the sunshine, into the courtyard of the castle. The heat seemed to be rising up from the cobblestones. The branches of the trees in the park hung heavy and the leaves were withered as if it hadn't rained for weeks, and in the middle of the courtyard the statue of the solitary man, weighed down by his bronze hat and the metallic folds of his raincoat, looked as if he were depicting some ancient sin, as impossible to hide on that bare pavement as the balls on a bulldog. 'This castle is just a fake,' I announced. 'No one has really lived their life here. It's just an illusion.' In the silence that followed, I added: 'Besides, the former owners committed suicide. And not even together. The man first, when he found out he was ruined, and then the woman in a hotel in Antwerp.'

Ghislaine nodded, not knowing whether I was making it up. 'Perhaps it's another fortress to breach,' she said, sounding ironic. So I invited her to come into town and have a drink on a café terrace. She hesitated, squinting as if she couldn't read me because of the sun in her eyes, but she said yes. And then there were four of us in my Peugeot. Behind us was Arnaud's Volkswagen Golf (he'd put his ballpoint in his shirt pocket) with little Elodie, whose white T-shirt caught my eye in the rear-view mirror. Two-thirds of the group was coming, which wasn't what I'd call intimate.

There was a canal running through the village, and the café terrace opened out onto a lawn beside the canal. It was as fresh and sparkling as a sorbet at the beach. Behind us, in the darkened interior, the blades of a fan flashed rhythmically as it hummed away on the counter. We talked a lot, light-heartedly, about nothing at all. When Ghislaine laughed, she leaned forward and I could see the colour of her eyes – a very pale blue, it was as if I could see the canal flowing in them – and the sweet little wrinkles that emphasised the corners. The years were weighing her down, I thought, and maybe I would too. I kept coming back to Bluebeard, and the fake castle, and the fake success.

Two men came and sat just in front of us on the terrace. From the back, one of them, fat and sweating, looked pretty repulsive to me with his glistening skull and the short curly hairs growing down over the rolls of fat at the nape of his neck. The other one, small and restless, made loud comments all the time and squirmed about on his chair. Then along came a much younger woman, smiling, looking relaxed behind her sunglasses, a woman who suddenly struck me as beautiful and funny, and sat down between the two of them. The sun slanted over them, shining on only one half of their table. So then this woman, talking and laughing, started massaging the fat man's neck. I could see her slender fingers gently working the folds of his flesh, I could feel the sweat beneath her hands as if it were mine and, despite telling myself she was just grooming a gorilla, I knew it felt good to him. I knew it so clearly, so deeply, it was overwhelming. The woman's fingers were hurting me. Cars were passing slowly by, almost soundless, and now in the fading afternoon an absolute calm descended, the colours took on their proper shades again: the flowers dozed in their sweet scent and night no longer needed to fall.

I was so insanely jealous that my ears started to buzz. When Ghislaine put down her glass of beer and looked up at me, her lips damp with froth, I stared hard into her pale blue eyes again. But the illusion had been shattered by the couple in front of us. It was completely lost, leaving in its place an immense, dizzying vacuum. I could see everything very clearly now. This tacky story, was that really what she liked? Bluebeard, Bluebeard and the key to success. The key? Well, if that's how it was, it would be me, not her, pocketing the profits. So I simply thanked her, thanked her for the exercise that had allowed me to write about my first lessons in love.

'Oh really?' she said, back to irony again. 'You've got someone who washes your dirty laundry?'

Everyone turned to look at me. And very quietly, I answered, 'Yes, you.'

VAN GOGH AT THE BATTLE OF ARLES

Our rooms – there were five on each side of the corridor,
I think – had been carved into the thick-walled silence.
Mine was like a monk's cell, but filled with light, and
through its narrow window I could look out onto a
garden in full bloom. The door swung shut behind
me; I ran my hand over its white painted surface, very
smooth, enjoying the coolness. The bed was high off
the floor, the desk was plain and square like a school
desk. I sat down on a pine chair and listened. In the
middle of the afternoon the place seemed completely
empty. Looking out the window again, I saw a corner
of the garden that had been laid out to look like one
of Van Gogh's paintings. This building in Arles where
the Literary Translators' Centre had been set up was
once a hospital, and even though the painter had had
his wounded ear cared for somewhere else, the whole
complex was named after him. The Provençal poet
Frédéric Mistral was another cultural hero ruling over
Arles, his portrait on display here and there. And for

a few days a third figure would come to haunt our retreat: Samuel Beckett. There was a conference on his work starting at the Centre, and Beckett translators were pouring in from every corner of the world.

Those of us who'd come here to finish a project in peace found ourselves caught up in the fizzing excitement of the conference, and vented our spleen at the disruption. The most outspoken was probably Radomir, a Serb writer and translator well known for his opposition to Milosevic. He came to France regularly in the belief that he'd be able to forget about the war, only to find himself all worked up in front of the TV, devouring the newspapers, railing against Western propaganda, trying to find his own space. He was what you'd call a good-looking guy, athletically built and sensitive at the same time, and he knew how to make the most of his charm. Everything was a target for his scathing irony, and the Beckett conference, which he referred to as a gathering of academic babblers, was no exception.

We enjoyed listening to him, maybe because of the brooding passion that coloured everything he said. On my very first evening there, out on the terrace where we liked to get together because it was unusually warm for late spring, I could feel something radiating from him, something restless, something that was probably burning him up. Sitting in our plastic armchairs, we would eat cherries and drink white wine, watching night fall over the town, always letting the same people carry the conversation. I don't know what it was I was hearing, I registered a buzzing of words and laughter while the swallows stitched across the infinite sky to the accompaniment of our chatter, and my mind dwelled on the mesh of words that would hold me for ever. A little while later the Austrian began to tell us the story of what he called his encounter with France. Spearing little cubes of goat cheese with the blade of his pocket knife, he waved them about while he held forth, like a conductor with his baton. Between statements he mouthed the cheese from his knife with a quick movement of his lips. His name was Jürgen and he had a reputation for being greener than the Greens. He was against the European Union for ecological reasons, and he'd driven down from the Tyrol, bringing with him in the back of his station wagon the bike he jumped on every morning to ride up one of the nearby hills. This time he was telling us a story from his student days in Nanterre – how some ageing priestess of post-structuralism had tried to have her way with him. When he got to the part where the old girl put her hand on his knee (we were in fits of laughter), I turned my head and Luisa caught my eye, a young Italian, inscrutable behind the delicate lenses of her glasses, a woman with such fair skin, especially in the faint evening light, that it was like the inside of some freshly cut fruit. And I sensed that her hand was about to slide across towards Jürgen's. He probably hadn't the slightest inkling. Does any man who's so articulate need to be able to read a woman's intentions?

★

Three days later, Jürgen fronted up around noon, still groggy with sleep and vowing he was going to get straight to work on a piece he was having trouble finishing. That was the morning Claes, the tall skinny Dutchman, with his cup of coffee in one trembling hand and a cigarette in the other, waggled his head in the direction of Jürgen's beautiful bike, propped in the entry-way. 'That's the end of the cycling,' he said in his gravelly voice, 'now there's Luisa.' Radomir nodded and added, 'It's all very well for Jürgen to give up his bike, but the problem is he's swapped *the book for the cover*.'

The 'cover' in question was the paper and bindings Luisa worked with in the Document Conservation Centre. For the past three years she'd been repairing books damaged by fires, floods and mildew or spoiled by foxing. Luisa, who must have been about twenty-five or so, worked in Bologna and Turin but came to Arles for three months every year. The centre where she worked was on the first floor of a huge and lovely old mansion. Her workshop there was a hospital for ailing manuscripts, parchments, printed documents, maps, old drawings and, of course, for wounded books. A refuge for the casualties of literature.

No sooner had Jürgen fallen for Luisa than he asked her to teach him her craft. He would join her in the evenings after her fellow workers had gone home. After her relationship with Jürgen started, Luisa didn't get to work before 2 or 3 pm, so she finished late, sometimes around 11 pm. When Jürgen turned up, they opened the windows, put on a cassette of baroque music and set to work. Jürgen would watch Luisa using the scissors and scalpel, cutting the leathers and that calfskin parchment she said you could only get now from a tiny village in northern Italy. He would copy what she was doing, learning from her example. He enjoyed using his hands, this man who worked so hard with his legs, riding his bike, and even harder with his head – he'd studied not just at Nanterre but in Vienna, Bologna and at Trinity College in Dublin as well.

Next came the glue and the brushes, the patches applied like bandages to the bare boards of the books, the chemicals applied to the ghostly writing revealing shadowy traces that seemed almost to be under the surface of the paper. Luisa worked with quick and careful precision, without speaking. Now and again Jürgen would take her in his arms and they would stand there, nestled against each other, then she would push him away, murmuring, 'I have to finish this book, just look at the mess the mildew has made.' And Jürgen, happy to see all these patients on the operating table, would nevertheless try to get Luisa to say, 'I bandaged the wounds, God healed them.' And this is how Jürgen, the first of us to leave his cell, was also the first to think he'd found heaven.

Radomir the Serb looked on their affair in a knowing way. He had first met Luisa during his stay the previous year, and had a rather special relationship with her. They would often talk together in private, and up until the Austrian's arrival, they used to eat pistachios and watch the TV news together. Now that she wasn't around any more, he couldn't make fun of French news headlines with her, or ridicule the intellectuals who held forth about the Balkans without knowing much about them. What's more, Radomir's closest friend, Claes, had no interest in politics whatsoever, and since a very reserved Croatian woman had just arrived the Serb preferred to keep his comments to himself. He moved on instead to finding more general targets for his irony, picking on the lordly poet Frédéric Mistral. Radomir found a new fault in him every day: this 'literary upstart' was for him the exact opposite of the gifted but struggling Van Gogh, and the embodiment of that Western specialty, propaganda. And this led him to the subject of the literatures of small countries. 'There are plenty of Faulkners in the Balkans,' he declared one evening. 'And even better writers. But they'll never be recognised.'

Yonghui, a round-faced Korean woman with a permanently innocent expression, asked him what he was talking about. Maybe she really didn't understand.

'He's defending Van Gogh against Mistral,' the Greek woman said, without taking her eyes from the TV screen.

This time I hoped Radomir would explain himself, but the door opened and the Dutchman Claes came in, or rather sidled slowly in. He was so gangly he just kept on coming through the doorway. And he was crying.

'Why are you crying?' Yonghui asked, getting to her feet.

But she was the only one to stand up. As far as the others were concerned, Claes had already drunk too much to be worth the effort.

'Oh boy, why am I crying?' Claes mimicked her. 'Well spotted!'

And he explained that a woman academic at the Beckett conference had called him a metaphysical tramp.

Radomir smiled into his glass of rosé.

We decided to wind up the evening at the bodega, where Jürgen and Luisa were going to join us, and so we set off happily through the streets. No more blue sky, just the scent of honeysuckle and the sound of our own footsteps. Claes complained that the bodega was too far away. He stared into every bar we passed as if that was his final destination, claiming he needed to make a phone call or buy cigarettes, but Radomir pulled him back with a firm hand and they came to a standstill only once, in front of the statue of Mistral, which Claes spat at a few times, only to have the *mistral* wind blow his spit right back at him.

When all six of us reached the bodega – Luisa and Jürgen had met up with us on the way – the waiters had already started to take in the tables and so we settled ourselves inside the bar. The owner was wearing a beret and a multicoloured sash, just as he used to when he was a matador; he rushed over to greet Claes, who was well known and well liked in most of the bars in town. Then, still holding on to Claes's hand, he bowed to Luisa and Yonghui. Actually, it would have been hard not to notice how beautiful they were. Straightening up again, he started talking about his prowess as a *torero* in Nîmes and Spain, where he'd worked with the very best. He told us about offering the bull's ears to his lady love in their bedroom after the bullfight, and Yonghui gazed at him with an expression of complete openness which he probably took for admiration. He was getting more and more carried away, his face flushed with excitement, and as he talked about his exploits the spittle flew. 'Two bottles of white for Table 3,' he shouted at length. 'On the house!' And he bowed again to Yonghui and Luisa, flourishing one arm as if he were waving a *muleta*. Then, taking a step back, with no warning and no guitar to accompany him, he burst into song, a tragic tale of love and death.

As he sang, I could see his throat bulging with the effort, the veins standing out as if preparing for the blow that would set them free, blood bursting forth, the *estocada*, the posthumous vengeance of the bulls he had lived off for so long, now coming back to get him, swelling up his throat in this braying love song. But it didn't kill him, and what saved him from death was good old married life. His wife, who'd been slaving away behind the bar for some time, took advantage of his pausing for breath to shout at him to stop playing the fool and come and give her a hand. He obeyed instantly, after one last bow, saluting us with his left arm in a final farewell.

Even the people at the nearby tables applauded.

In all this racket, I turned to look at Radomir, whose face was flushed in the reflected candlelight – only one eye and his curly blond hair were visible – and asked him why he and Claes had spat at the statue of Mistral. Claes, fine, I could understand that (the drink was always an excuse), but why him? He leaned back, his mouth stretching into a broad grin, and when he leaned forward again he asked, 'I can tell them, can't I, Luisa?', nudging her gently with his elbow.

And Luisa, looking embarrassed, answered, 'Sure, go ahead', and turned away at once towards Jürgen, already on his feet to go for cigarettes.

Very quietly, making us lean closer to him, Radomir told us that a few months earlier Luisa had found an unpublished letter from Vincent Van Gogh to his brother Theo. A letter that was going to be published, now that it had been authenticated by a Dutch expert.

'The letter had been glued inside the cover of a book to strengthen it,' Luisa explained. 'That wasn't unusual at the start of the century.'

'It's astounding!' Radomir thundered. 'His paintings were used to plug up holes in chicken coops, and his letters to stick torn books back together.'

'A universal quick-fix?' asked Yonghui.

'Like duct tape,' Jürgen said, offering Luisa one of his Camel Lights.

He must have known about it already because he didn't seem to react at all to what we were saying.

'I did my master's on Van Gogh, I'm interested in this,' growled Claes.

'The important part,' continued Radomir, 'is what's in the letter, which was never posted. It's about Van Gogh's visit to Mistral in the spring of 1888. What it is,' he stressed, 'is proof the two men met. Mistral was already famous, even if he hadn't won the Nobel Prize yet. Van Gogh says that Mistral treated him with contempt, thinly disguised behind a barrage of typically southern effusiveness. And in the letter he also repeats Gauguin's statement that Arles is the dirtiest place in the South of France.'

My jaw dropped.

'Well, gotta go,' said Luisa.

'You can't,' I insisted, 'you've got to tell us the whole thing.'

'Radomir knows more about it than I do,' she said with a faint smile.

And off they went, she and Jürgen, disappearing down the little street, two tall slender figures, twined around each other like vines.

'Ain't love wonderful,' Radomir jeered. 'But fame and fortune are better.'

Their offhandedness left me stunned. To walk out on us like that after such a revelation! I let go of Yonghui — I'd grabbed her arm without realising. She seemed more amused by our discussion, by the looks on our faces, than by the possible implications of the discovery.

'Hey, Radomir,' Claes asked, 'why did Van Gogh go to see Mistral? The prince of poets and the pariah, they don't mix.'

'Maybe they do,' Radomir answered.

'And it was after that that Vincent cut off his ear, right?' spluttered Claes. He had tears in his eyes at the thought of it as he held his glass in mid-air, unable to drink from it or put it down. Through his tears he must have had a pretty distorted view of the world.

Radomir shrugged. He didn't know, and in a way all these details were pointless. At that precise moment I felt a kind of grace floating above us. In this nearly empty bodega with dirty sawdust on the floor and bits of paper blowing along the street, with the half-empty bottles and the fatigue of the evening enveloping everything, even the last notes of some distant music, I had the impression that we hadn't come to Arles by accident, that we'd been secretly summoned to the Translation Centre to witness real justice being done, justice that would bridge the centuries, justice that would mean the Van Goghs of this world would never again turn their razors or their guns against themselves but against their oppressors instead. And this letter, the weapon Van Gogh hadn't dared to use, one of us was going to wield it for him.

We wanted to know more. Who did the letter belong to? Was Luisa entitled to publish it in some national paper the way she intended to? Who would get the money?

Bit by bit, at the bodega to begin with, then as we walked along the banks of the Rhône, Radomir answered our questions as best he could, but always with a certain reserve that I found extremely irritating.

I pictured Luisa opening an old book that had water damage, a volume of poetry in the Provençal language (this would be the best way to introduce Van Gogh's opposition to Mistral); she'd noticed the folded-over page reinforcing the cover. Lifting back a corner of it, she saw the pencilled signature, *Vincent*. Maybe she thought of Van Gogh at that point. In any case, she decided to save the document and tried to detach it gently, by steaming it. When this didn't work, because the glue had soaked too deeply into the paper, she had to use the scalpel to free the two pages by cutting the cover away from beneath them. And there, under the transparent yellow layer of glue, was a three-page letter written in pencil, addressed to Theo, signed and dated. And never sent.

Why not? Perhaps because it was destined to reach her, Luisa, over a hundred years later, one September evening when she would be alone in her workshop, so alone that there'd be no one to call 'Come and look at this!' to, and so she'd turn towards the other maimed books, the pages laid out to dry or pinned to the wall, waving in the breeze as if they were trying to respond. Because real post, real letters between people who know how to speak and how to listen, are vague fumblings, full of awkwardness and the vagaries of chance.

Oh, how Luisa's head must have swum with it! And what was she going to do now with this treasure?

'Tell me, Radomir, how did she manage to hold on to this letter? I mean . . .'

Claes, wandering along behind us, had started to compose a poem. We could hear him intoning:

Plane trees
symmetrical lanterns
Frédéric Mistral's back

He called out 'Vincent', then a few paces further 'poor man', as if he'd tripped on the first word and caught himself from falling on the next ones, his stumbling walk matching the rhythm of his words.

Radomir had drifted off onto general topics, describing Arles as the central pivot of the compass, the embryonic heart of European culture, where the confrontation between Mistral and Van Gogh foreshadowed our own. I'm pretty sure he said 'our own', in any case he went on about good and evil, about how American soaps, with their simplistic oppositions, had become the template of Western education.

'Like the opposition between Van Gogh and Mistral,' I exclaimed. 'Here we are smack in the middle of a cultural soap opera.'

'Uh huh,' he said, sniggering, 'now you're starting to get it.'

He stopped. I could feel the cold at my back, the wind blowing off the Rhône. I tried to look Radomir in the eye, saw his face like a statue's, glistening and rigid. Yonghui, beside me, was staring at him too.

'Don't go getting all worked up about it,' he said. 'You either, Yonghui.'

'Why not?'

'There is no letter,' Radomir said. 'I made it up.'

A brief pause, then he added, 'With Luisa's agreement.'

For a moment there was no sound but our breathing.

'I was talking to Luisa about *the injustice of history* when the idea came to me,' he said.

Claes came up to us. He was listening too, but he didn't seem to have caught on yet.

'Oh, come on,' Radomir told me, 'don't look at me like that. Can't you feel it now, *the injustice of history*?'

Oh yes, I could feel it all right! It was pounding in my ears. I put my hands over them. There was a hissing pain drilling into my head, amplifying the noise of the wind and the Rhône. And Radomir, arrogant as a lord in the face of my frowning expression, saying to Claes, 'It would have been really great if the letter had existed. Don't you think that's weird? Don't you think it's weird that we put so much . . . passion into justifying our little obsessions? It disgusts me.' And he spat. But since he spat with the *mistral*, nothing rebounded back at him.

I shouted, 'You used Van Gogh, that's despicable!'

He stopped, looking at me sideways. He was much bigger and stronger than me, and not over-impressed by my anger. He was probably even pleased about it.

'Oh, come off it,' he answered. 'That's what art is. If you're going to create, you have to know how to lie.'

Claes put his head in his hands, groaning. 'That's crazy, man. Yeah, I thought as much. Something didn't ring true.'

'You suspected something!' I exclaimed, totally disgusted.

Yonghui, meanwhile, had withdrawn into a dense and silent hostility.

A little further on, Radomir started to whistle softly between his teeth.

'You'll be able to write about this,' he said, turning to me, his teeth gleaming whitely in the moonlight.

THE SLAVE GAME

Because of the heat inside, all those bodies dancing to the music, I had to slip out once in a while to get a breath of frosty air. A light near the door glowed golden on the last leaves of the vine on the trellis. In our shirt sleeves, with our cheeks on fire, four or five of us were catching our breath, enjoying the little clouds that puffed out of our mouths when we spoke, like in a comic. There was a big pink neon sign on the roof of the house across the street. I couldn't take my eyes off it as it turned slowly in the night: RESTAURANT LEMOINE – 01 64 25 7   22. Especially the black hole between the 7 and the 22, where the number had been sucked up by the darkness or eaten away by the mist that rose from the fields and clung to the sign like a long white train – a queen's veil drifting over the houses crouched beneath the frost.

When my teeth started to chatter, I crushed my cigarette against the pillar and went back inside to the uproar of the party.

The evening was winding down, towards midnight, when Jean-Luc and Sylvie took the accordions out of their blue velvet-lined cases. Their fingers pressed the mother-of-pearl buttons, and the purply bellows began to swell and deflate like toads' throats. Shouting *an dro,* the dancers held hands and circled lightly – like korrigan goblins in their pointed clogs – moving faster and faster, whirling about, losing our inhibitions. The dance drew us into its crucible, hammered at us, annihilated us, sucked the breath out of us. Our bodies grew hot, sweaty, shiny. When it reached melting-point, the dance broke down into ingots, as people paired off. One of these couples stood out, love glowing on the face of Lise as she gazed at her partner Jeannot. She'd thrown caution to the wind, forgotten everything else, her cheeks and forehead were calm and sleek. She was drinking in the look in Jeannot's eyes, and what we could see in hers sent a shiver of envy down our spines. Jeannot was leaning towards her, smiling, his eyes half-closed and his chin tucked down against the front of his Mexican shirt. He was so entranced that even his trouser legs were quivering. Over beside the sink, Lise's husband was tossing salad in a big white glass bowl. Now and again he would shake his head, flicking his ponytail as if to shoo away some insect, and look with a glazed expression in the direction of the two dancers, not really seeing them. Then he would grip the long wooden spoon tightly and stuff his mouth full of salad. Here, anchored in his ordinariness, he was the husband and nothing more.

Jeannot was married too: his wife was bobbing about energetically, like an electric rabbit, in front of her placid partner. She had a red ribbon in her hair, tied in a bow like two big ears.

Once the dance had finished, I withdrew into a darker corner, near Adeline, a very tall young woman who hadn't joined the circle. She was sitting on the couch, staring into space, stroking the cushion on her knee. Her face seemed so soft, so malleable, it was as if it hadn't quite taken on solid form yet. But her features were well defined, well shaped, with a proud, almost horse-like expression. When she stood up, it wasn't so much an unfolding as an uncoiling: her back and her bare arms rose endlessly up and up. She began to dance by herself, moving in sensuous circles that made my skin, my eyes and my mouth tingle. How I longed to be in love too, to float away, to have eyes for no one but Adeline. I was only too aware that this group of people, *our* group, as soon as it stopped whipping itself along, working itself into a froth and a fever, was a complete mess, a spoiled mayonnaise, a saturated solution of everyday habits. Those who were married were unhappily married, those who were on their own were unhappily on their own, only this white-hot fever kept us going.

This quivering I called desire was exactly what I'd felt standing outside in the cold looking at the restaurant's illuminated sign. Earlier on, the whole morning, I'd felt *contented for no reason*, with a kind of general tendency towards happiness, my compass turning aimlessly, looking for the lost north. And here I was tonight, in this room in a distant suburb burning in the middle of the frozen landscape, with my needle pointing straight at Adeline, alone among the couples.

But it was only after several long minutes that I dared to exchange with her the kind of meaningful looks that were straight out of a silent movie: greasepaint looks, complete with arched eyebrows, pouty mouths and cheeks sucked in. She responded with an equally comical attitude that seemed to be saying, 'The initial attraction is better than the follow-up.' So I went out into the parking area and dived into the cold. It was too dark to see my breath, but I lit a cigarette, taking occasional puffs, and gazed again at the illuminated sign for the Restaurant Lemoine. I had the feeling I knew more about this giant pink sign, indifferent to cold and solitude. I would have liked to bring it down to my level. And then what? Take it in my arms, comfort it? And then what? Smash it and throw it away like a broken toy? Walking slowly towards my car, I noticed a couple: a woman whose name I couldn't remember with some other woman's husband. They were so drunk they were falling over each other as they kissed; they pushed each other away, struggling to stay upright, then staggered to one side and came back to fumble again.

I thought about Adeline. One shared look had sufficed to seal the deal: desire, simple desire with no future to it. Play the game and suffer the consequences. And yet I would have sworn she was the kind of girl who would have on her wall (or engraved in her mind) 'It is better to have loved and lost than never to have loved at all.'

When I went back inside the auction had started. The room was on the boil. They had pulled the table into the middle, and the women had already taken up position around it.

They hung numbers around our necks. I was 8, the number written in orange on a rectangle of cardboard cut from a carton. Music played solemnly, some kind of wedding or military march replacing the rock and roll. The bank, represented by Véronique – also nominated as auctioneer because she actually worked at the Indo-Suez Bank – was handing out a thousand francs of Monopoly money to each woman. Through trades and resales, that sum would quickly change. Some women would find themselves handling a larger amount, but no slaves; others would have two or three men but be broke or in debt. The fourteen male slaves, one of them Clothilde's young brother – stunningly pale, he couldn't have been more than fifteen – were shuffling their weight from one foot to the other, swapping jokey comments. A man in a blue velvet shirt whose name I didn't know, pretty far gone already, was announcing himself as the deal of the century. I waved my label about gently, like a cowbell; I thought it was just as charming and just as deeply horrible.

'Who'll tell us about Number 3's good points?' auctioneer Véronique asked, pointing at Jeannot.

Answers fired back: he burns the pasta, he can't iron, he's good with figures, he's got sexy arms, etc. His wife, the little hoppity rabbit with the red ribbon, came right out and said he had a secret vice and she wouldn't pay a single cent for him, personally. Lise, still in love with Jeannot, mumbled a few unintelligible words, and in the end didn't have the nerve to choose him. For six hundred francs, he was sold off in the first round to another stable, where he was asked to sing for the group. He fidgeted for a moment, and had barely started a song by Boby Lapointe that he didn't really know the melody to, not to mention the words, when he was interrupted by applause and promises that he'd be bought back in the second round.

Because it's in the resale round that things get serious. When the buyers total up what they've got left. 'I'm putting Number 8 up for sale again,' Régine shouted, pounding the table with her fist. Number 8, me. No one flinched, no one raised the bid. 'You're stuck with him, girl,' Marie murmured; she'd just acquired a young lad, promising to put him through the mill. 'My thousand francs are gone already because of you,' she told him. 'How can I go on playing? Go and get us something to drink, now, you need to work to earn your keep.'

Tall and swaying, Adeline was muttering to herself, as if she were humming a song, cupping her hand around the hidden banknotes. She'd already picked little Guillaume, and called out in a loud voice, 'Four hundred francs for Number 8, Henri.'

'That's a hundred less than I paid for him,' Régine answered. 'I want six hundred!'

Adeline leaned towards Lise, trying to borrow from her the two hundred francs she didn't have. Lise, who still wanted to acquire Jeannot, hesitated. 'I have to get some money, too,' she said. Jeannot had just gone up to twelve hundred: a luxury item, top of the range, Véronique announced, while Jeannot, in his loose cotton pants, smiled blissfully. Lise carried on with her calculations. She looked at Paul, her husband, so thin and pinched-looking with his skimpy ponytail. She said in a neutral voice, 'I'm borrowing four hundred from the bank and I'm putting Number 2 up for sale.'

Number 2 was Paul. Unmoved, he lit a cigarette.

Lise was still waiting for a response from the bank to her request for a loan.

'Who wants to lend to Lise?' asked banker Véronique.

Hardly anyone looked up. Deals were being worked out in whispers. Plots were being hatched. The laughing faces from earlier in the evening were becoming expressionless. Men were still changing hands.

Véronique rapped her wooden gavel and repeated her question.

No response.

So Véronique decided to give Lise a loan 'on the bank'. 'It's a takeover,' Marie shouted, adding amid all the hubbub, 'The bank is colluding with lovers!' But Véronique stood firm, and that's how Jeannot, who'd done nothing up till then except smile, found himself close to Lise. Which was as it should be. Straight away, Adeline asked Lise for the two hundred francs she had left over, and bought me. The atmosphere thickened. People were losing track of who owed what to whom, and Marie set both her men free, swearing they were worth less than the paper the Monopoly money was printed on.

I found myself sitting on Adeline's left while little Guillaume was lording it with his usual smugness. He winked, flapped his cardboard label about, pulled at the mother-of-pearl buttons on his red waistcoat and entertained himself by tickling Adeline's ribs; she didn't react. Because he can't suckle her breasts, I thought. And I shook my head scornfully.

'So then,' Adeline said, turning suddenly towards me, 'is someone jealous of his little brother? But actually you're the youngest in the family.'

I forced an embarrassed smile. Even sitting down, Adeline towered over us. She was sweating a bit, and when I pressed my nose against her shoulder, I could pick the sweat beneath her perfume.

At that point I felt deeply sad. As if we couldn't help it, we had to sit there, she and I, glued together like this, raising our heads to take a breath and then diving back down. My neck was gripped by a terrible cramp. My mouth twisted but I didn't manage to shout anything, and I almost abandoned Adeline to sprawl across the table. The pain didn't last long, though, just left me with the feeling of a caress gone wrong. I sat up straight, smiling again.

I had always wanted to believe that it would be a horribly difficult thing to do, to sleep with my mother. But I felt fine, sitting on one of Adeline's knees. Astride the rump of the world. Just as insolent as Guillaume.

'Well,' she said, 'the two of you are going to sing for us.'

It was when we found ourselves standing there side by side, that horrible little runt Guillaume and I, that it was the hardest for me. Our cardboard labels bumped together and swung apart, beating out a sort of voiceless tune and not even forming a wall between us. And all those people staring brazenly at our faces, shouting out: 'They must know a lullaby at least!'

Adeline chuckled, and got up to find herself something to drink. I wished I could disappear into a pack of cards, I'd be the eight of diamonds. In his red waistcoat, Guillaume thought he was still the joker. And then, although we hadn't managed to produce even the slightest sound, people were turning casually away from us, conversations started up again about who had won or lost, the good deals and the bad.

Adeline came back. She was holding a glass of sparkling water, so fizzy the bubbles were making her hand wet.

'Singing water,' she said. 'It's singing for you.'

I asked her if I could stick my finger in it, just to feel its coolness. But I did it without waiting for her to answer. The glass fell from her hand and exploded on the parquet floor. A few sharp-edged pieces projected pale reflections into the water, sparkling with the last of its energy. I would have liked to lean over this little glinting world, to read my future in it.

Adeline's mouth was an O of surprise. She stood stock still, contemplating the life escaping between the segments of parquet. Who was it who said that dreams shatter like glass?

A voice talked about turning on the light, cleaning up, not cutting yourself. It was slow, unbearably slow. I could feel my feet sticking to the floor.

'I'm out of here,' I said.

I got rid of my label, or rather I tore it up, into two pieces to start with, then, once I was outside, into four, then into shreds. I threw them in front of me, pathetic little paving stones that I crushed underfoot as I went, breathing in the frosty air, spitting but not trying to put out the fire that was burning down the house.

THE IMMORTALS

We'd been travelling in this bus for quite a while and weren't looking at the scenery any more, maybe because all the bumping about was putting us to sleep; then the Belgian Guy started talking about Corsican donkeys. To start with it was just a vague rumbling, I could make out only a few stray expressions – holidays, the middle of summer – then the word 'castration' made us sit up and take notice. He was saying that he'd heard the donkey braying the whole night long. Even stuffing his fingers right into his ears he still couldn't block the noise out – let alone get to sleep. In the morning when he went into the field he found the donkey tied up to a tree, its neck rubbed raw from trying to pull itself free, but what was really painful to see was the string tied around its testicles, so tight it was practically slicing them off: they were so swollen and purple they looked like eggplants ready to explode. The farmer defended his actions: 'Normally it don't hurt 'em, but this critter's a bit different,' and concluded that he should have done the job the usual way, tying the donkey's balls off as tight as possible, then crushing them between a couple of stones. Sure, it would hurt at the time, but a couple of hours later it'd be all over, completely forgotten.

I remember I assured the Belgian Guy it was absolutely, positively true, you do forget everything because remembering's too painful, but someone else shrugged and said that people aren't donkeys. The Retired Professor turned around – he was listening to everything from two rows away – and said with a sneer that castration isn't all that straightforward, he felt almost embarrassed at having to explain it. 'What it means,' he said, tilting his chin, 'is accepting that you won't become who you are.'

'Is that right?' We nodded, but rolled our eyes. And yet the Professor had opted to come to the mountains with us, not go with the others on a pilgrimage to Lourdes so that the Virgin would keep them fighting fit. Well, I've known him for quite a while and I can definitely say he's no better than the rest of us, especially the nonsense he spouts.

Georges, the one we call the eternal working man because of his vinyl bag, stuck his head up over the back of White Hat's seat and launched into some story about his cousin who for years had spent every weekend doing up his beach house to retire to. He'd built a really fancy bathroom upstairs, and then blow me down if a month before they were set to move in he didn't go and have a heart attack. He'd got over it, but no way could he carry on with the renovations or even go upstairs, he'd had to sell the place and stay in his flat in the suburbs with his wife, who wouldn't speak to him any more. 'Yeah, so what's that got to do with castration?' Black T-shirt wanted to know – he always liked to have things spelled out for him.

It wasn't the theory we were interested in, but how painful it is when they're cut off, because that way we could squeeze our thighs together and laugh and that made us feel as though we still had balls, even if at other times we had let someone else wear the trousers and said, 'Next time we'll see who's boss', and then when the next time came we hadn't even noticed.

I'm an insurance agent with a nice little retirement nest egg, I'm the one who loudly proclaimed that castration is quite painless. So it was my idea, not White Hat's – he started in straight away talking about how dangerous holiday homes are, with some really convoluted story about a priest, no, not a priest, a churchgoer who became a priest after an accident. So anyway this churchgoer, he pottered around every weekend fixing up his beach house, but he was sleeping with some woman there as well, even though he was married, and one afternoon there was a terrible storm and a beam fell onto the lovers' bed and the guy was killed instantly. Several of us in the bus shook our heads. Some people didn't believe a word of it because White Hat, well . . . But mostly we pointed out to him that, if his guy was dead, there wasn't too much chance of him getting to be a priest. So then White Hat went red in the face, started shouting that sure you could, we'd see, you can be all kinds of things when you're dead, and the more he went on about it the more we laughed, till finally he admitted it wasn't the dead guy who became a priest, it was the husband of the woman in the bed with him. That bit too, it wasn't all that clear, poor old Hat, you forgot the most important part, and Black T-shirt, taking a drag on his cigarette, mumbled, 'Hardly surprising the government we've got when you think guys like him have the vote.' Prof couldn't help sticking his oar in, commenting that it was inevitable someone would bring up a priest when the topic was castration, and that was really what Hat meant. That shut us up for about ten seconds, while White Hat cracked a grin, like, 'See, you guys, I'm more clued up than you think,' and what happened later proved he wasn't too far wrong about that, even with his story about some dead guy heaps of things kept happening to.

We were still trying to work our way out of this, to hang on to the idea that we could have the comforts of death and yet still be alive, and this came from the bumping along, our tiredness, digesting our heavy midday meal and especially from the habit, the well-established habit, of being regulated from the outside, by the ticking of the clock and the cycle of repeated gestures. Our heads wobbled against the headrests, we'd closed our eyes, some of us were snoring, the bus travelled on, braking as it entered the curves and vrooming out of them, skidding slightly sideways – the world was carrying us away and all was well.

When we stepped down off the bus towards six in

the evening, the reflected glow of the sky was lighting up the mountainside. The grass was smooth and dry, the colour of the broom bushes had dulled as if they were refusing to display their brightness, and all five of us leaned against the parapet looking out over the valley. We were all dressed the same, short-sleeved T-shirt and cotton sunhat. We'd all put our cameras on the low wall and we were waiting, cigarettes in the corners of our mouths. What we were waiting for was hard to say. You might have thought we were posing for a photo, but in fact we were planning to take one.

I knew exactly what taking a photo meant, that moment when you step out of the present and into an unreal future, when you freeze-frame yourself in full flight heading nowhere, and in any case nothing was moving in this landscape, not even the people on the beach down below. A man-made beach, most likely, with painted plaster statues of the kind they used to make in those days with the idea of putting art into the natural environment. Which really bugged me, because we'd had just about enough of human beings, their so-called achievements as well as their endless chatter.

Nevertheless, we'd managed to stop talking. Even when the driver disturbed our drowsiness, we got off without making any big speeches, barely a few grunts, as though each of us was still caught up in his own dream, and the driver hadn't felt the need to bawl at us as he usually did, 'Come on, get a move on, you'll miss the panoramic view, from the corniche you can see the sea to the west, hurry up, Mr Terrone, step lively, look at Mr Lesourd, blah blah blah.' Sometimes he made do with a cassette that brayed a tourist commentary through the bus.

We waited, in silence. The heat sang in our ears, the ground dropped away beneath us, lizards slipped between our feet and disappeared further down in the reddish sand. Our cigarettes burned away in the corners of our mouths without our dragging on them. It was as though we didn't need to breathe any more.

I had pins and needles in my legs already when Georges, the eternal working man, scratched at his grey moustache and muttered that he knew that family. He meant the bathers in front of us, a woman in a green swimsuit that struggled to contain her enormous belly. Sitting there, thighs apart, she was sucking at a huge cone piled with purple ice-cream – raspberry, blackcurrant, or just colouring? The other woman, her hair dyed red, was standing there in a red and yellow-flowered swimsuit, apparently looking out to sea. Between them, the skinny bald man, not a hair on his skull or chest, was bent over his notebook. With the sun shining full on his face and cooking him like a brick, he looked like a traditional Egyptian scribe, and that touched me because I thought he looked like me. I'd done that too, bent over ledgers for years, only I would never have dared to go to the office in a bathing suit. But at the office I'd dreamed of spending all eternity at the beach, yes I had, as long as I wouldn't be hungry or cold there.

Georges said again, nearly in tears, that he knew

these people really well, they'd been away on holiday together. Sometimes-Paul (because he often changed his name) said he that knew the Baldies, and Black T-shirt added that the man's spindly legs and the ladies' fat thighs, it was proof they were real, because that's what happens over the years, the fat transfers from the man to the woman, it seals their union over time, they are one flesh though their souls go in different directions, one drifts off to some dream life, the other into the jumbled world of magazines.

We kept our eyes fixed on these characters, and I remember a bittersweet regret took hold of me, it's a silly thing to say because I didn't even know what any of this had to do with me, I'd always despised my job in insurance – and that poor scribe, over there! We couldn't look away any more, there was no point even in trying to lift up our cameras. I wanted to get rid of my nostalgia, I said the word, but even the word had started to gnaw at me, and that was when the thought came to me that nostalgia is desire that has lost its teeth: where else did it leave them if not in my flesh, complete with their fillings and other ballast that weighs me down, turns my legs to clay, to posts like the ones on that lifeguard behind the Baldy family (he's standing there, his hands up to his forehead for protection from the sun, which is actually shining on his *back* – isn't that ridiculous? – and he's sunk into the sand halfway up his calves, but he doesn't notice that any more than he does the paint that's peeling off his cheeks).

To say we were fascinated would be an understatement. Even White Hat couldn't open his mouth, his tongue had got too heavy. It came over us quietly, like permanent peace, and, I repeat, painlessly. Then our ears closed, our cares flew away, we had won the last battle.

A truck passed close by us with such a fearful racket that we trembled on our bases.

'Did it crack my spinal column?' asked Georges. 'Can you see any soil leaking out?'

He got an answer a long time later. From now on we needed a lot of patience to put together the shortest sentence.

'Soon,' Sometimes-Paul said, 'we'll be just little piles of soil with poppies growing out of us.'

'You can't know that it'll be poppies,' the Belgian Guy said slowly, 'you won't have any choice.'

A sparrow perched on his head and it wasn't until after it had flown away that the Belgian Guy carried on, 'That's why you don't know what it will be, because you won't have any choice.'

'*Non sequitur,*' said Prof, whose skin had turned quite green, '*non sequitur.*'

There were young men tearing down the slope at great speed. The heat was at its fiercest, even the cliffs were sweating and the figurines of painted clay looked as though they were surrounded by a halo of steam.

'Hey,' called a boy with long blond hair, 'look!'

He'd pulled up behind the five little statues and put

one finger on the Belgian Guy's shoulder, scratching at the paint.

'No dust,' he said, 'it must have rained recently.'

A stocky, muscular girl wearing shorts, sweating beneath her backpack, popped up beside him. She was followed by a tall dark lad. Sweat glistened on their faces and they were puffing noisily, still out of breath. Speaking with a southern French accent that gave a kind of mocking tone to his words, the dark boy exclaimed:

'They're *santons*!'*

'That'll be the day,' the girl answered, unscrewing the top of her water bottle.

Then they sat down amongst the broom bushes. The pebbles in the dry earth made them fidget about from time to time. The statuettes lined up along the low wall were facing away from them and they could see part of the beach and its occupants.

Alexis, the blond one, was the first to get up and explore the surroundings. He plunged into the bushes, a stick in one hand as if he were afraid of snakes, and came across a wooden sign a few metres in, its blue-painted letters reading END OF TRAIL. On the left, a little shelter had been built, a miniature replica of a Metro station with its porcelain tiles and panel of enamelled steel saying RÉPUBLIQUE. A little old man

* *Translator's note*: Santons are small ornamental figures, which are manufactured in the South of France and often represent village people – the baker, the butcher, etc. They are also used in Christmas nativity scenes.

with very wrinkly skin was standing there, wearing a battered brown felt hat and metal-rimmed glasses. But his wrinkles weren't unattractive, they looked like the effects of lifelong happiness. So he was one of those *sweet little old men* that you see in picture books, not much connection with the stupid old sods I know, Alexis decided. The idea of the *sweet little old man,* which he repeated to himself, was starting to annoy him intensely.

'Come and see,' he shouted, 'we've got a nativity scene in the woods!'

Only the dark lad, whose name was Max, made a move. He smiled at the sight of the statuette and the model of the Metro station.

'What d'you reckon, maybe it's an allegory of the Republic,' he said. 'What a laugh.'

'What d'you reckon,' Alexis repeated, taking the mickey. 'Easy to say. Someone must have used these clay dolls as a setting and left them behind. Nature as garbage dump!'

'A setting for what?' Max asked.

'Who knows? There's nutters everywhere, people who deface graves, solstice worshippers, what do I know?'

'Irène's not wrong when she says you're all wound up.'

'She said that? What made her say that?'

'I wonder,' grunted Max.

Alexis didn't pursue the question, instead he went a bit deeper into the undergrowth. He was angry with

Irène because she was in love with him and didn't dare admit it.

When they met up again, Alexis mentioned his dislike of this tasteless theatre again. Irène talked about ancient art, Easter Island, Middle Eastern fertility statuettes.

'You see what I was saying,' Alexis said to Max.

'No, what were you saying?'

'As soon as someone gives a scholarly name to something cretinous, it stops being cretinous.'

Irène didn't take the bait.

'What intrigues me,' she said, 'is that they've got those clay cameras. As if someone wanted to depict tourists. The ones who were going to capture it on film have been captured themselves.'

Alexis shrugged and moved off again. Max and Irène lay down in the silence punctuated by insects, the light breeze, the occasional rumble of a distant car. Then they heard the sound of branches breaking, a figurine being knocked over. It was the old man from the Metro station. Irène got up on her hands and knees and spotted through the bushes a hiking boot with its white sock and calf muscle covered in blond hairs glistening in the sun. The whole thing crushed the back of the Pauper with a cracking sound like a splintering carapace.

'Yuk,' they heard Alexis's voice, 'my foot's covered in gunk.'

'You shouldn't have done that,' said Max.

'You're so gross,' Irène shouted.

'These things are an insult to the environment,' responded Alexis.

When he reappeared, a smile of satisfaction was floating on his lips. 'Shall we go now?' he asked. 'We've got another six k's before we get there.'

But the others were offended and pretended he hadn't said anything. They stayed sitting, watching the sun sink towards the plain, shining brightly on the little beach and its eternal holiday-makers. Bees arrived on a sudden breeze, zigzagging past their noses. Their hives must have been behind the derelict house on the far side of the lavender field.

After a while, Irène pulled a towel out of her backpack and lay down on it. The sky seemed to be turning purple, as if it was filling with paint.

'My body!' she cried out.

'What about your body?' Max asked limply, inspecting his toes.

'It's so heavy, so stiff.'

'It's all the exercise,' said Max.

'I feel like a female truck,' Irène said.

'A truck,' Max laughed. 'Vroom, vroom.'

'Oh no, not a truck,' Alexis said. 'Maybe a Mis-Truck.'

'Thanks,' Irène said flatly. 'Mis-Truck suits me fine.'

She looked at the sky again through the still branches.

Max got to his feet, crossed the road and stepped over the low wall, took off his shirt and trousers and lay down on his side. Shading his eyes from the sun, he could make out a fat dark-haired woman licking at a raspberry ice-cream. Sitting beside her was a brick-coloured man, his shoulders hunched, absorbed in reading a catalogue: he looked like an Egyptian scribe. A little further to the left, on a level with the screen fence made of reeds, a middle-aged blonde was stretched out on a towel, a silent transistor in front of her, reading a rain-faded book. Max scrutinised her rounded rump, barely covered by a pink bikini bottom, her exposed breasts and her big hair – a helmet of combed blond clay whorls and twirls, a pathetic imitation of the Gorgon's fatal charms. He'd met this woman hundreds of times, at the beach and in offices, a lonely and disenchanted employee who could have been his mother. And was his mother, even.

And last but not least, near the waves and a wooden bathing shed, the handsome lifeguard with his hands shading his eyes from the sun. The wind and the birds had worn away his Speedos and nibbled off a bit of his penis, leaving a grey mark at that spot.

Max's mother was a teacher, she'd often taken him to a beach like this one, and the bald man's trio could have been his uncle and aunts. He relaxed into the sand, let the sun caress him. Trying to watch a bee that was hovering around him, he remembered something he'd seen on TV: the image of a bee laden with pollen struggling against the wind. He couldn't see the bee, just an image that made him think he could.

★

Alexis was in a foul mood, he was already bad-tempered when he knocked over the Pauper, but it was worse now because the others were making such a big deal out of it. He thought about taking off on his own, decided it would be childish and undid his pack to get something to eat. A can of beer rolled across the pebbles. It was warm, it would spray in all directions if he opened it. He realised now that he'd made a mistake in bringing it. But in the mountains aren't there supposed to be streams with really cold water to chill the beer? Wasn't that as normal as sea water being salty? This mountain wasn't right. Unrolling a balled-up T-shirt, he took out a wedge of bread cut from a round loaf and some cow's-milk cheese, as soft and pliable as anyone could wish.

Oh, the simple pleasure of eating out of doors, on a hike or a wander through the fields, of *breaking bread* as they used to say in the days when bread had a crust to break. And this evening, wouldn't it have been great to sleep beside a rushing river, right next to Irène? Not that he was in love with her, he told himself, but if there was a girl around, he didn't like it if she didn't pay more attention to him. Irène had a problem, for sure. Because everywhere he went, women were waiting just for him, even women he'd never seen before: they just recognised him, that was all. Like the week before, that pretty waitress in the bar in the Hôtel des Trois Montagnes, who said she was a student and left him her room number in the saucer with the bill. The Lady Blanchefleur welcoming her knight Percival.

That was his greatest satisfaction, discovering that

things can actually happen the way they do in an ancient legend and that life could be as predictable as a Hollywood film: wasn't that the only way to find justice? Those who were born beautiful should lead beautiful lives, the under-endowed should live out their mediocre existences, and all would be well in the world. A principle neither Max nor Irène accepted. But was it within their power to escape this rule?

The Gypsy in the Oasis Bar would have been in complete agreement with him. They had met her four days earlier on the beach of a murky bay with rotting tree trunks crashing together in the waves. She held her sessions in the back room, her chanting punctuated by the lapping of the muddy water and the sound of people slapping at mosquitoes. Smiling with secret disdain, Alexis let her turn over the cards, *pretending* to believe in it, not realising until later that pretending or believing amounted to exactly the same thing.

The Gypsy turned up the Wanderer, with his stick on his shoulder and his bundle tied to the end of it. He had long grey hair. 'That's you when you're older,' she said.

'I'd have preferred Sir Lancclot of the Lake, or La Hire, Joan of Arc's right-hand man,' Alexis joked.

'He's also called the Wandering Fool,' the woman said, 'you'll know why.'

'How much do I owe you?' Alexis asked, to put an end to it.

She held out the back of her hand to him, as if he was supposed to kiss it. He looked at the rings, the wrinkled, sun-browned skin, and leaned forward, still smiling, to touch his lips to the hand. His blond hair, like a Renaissance Christ's, spread across the woman's forearm. Then, lifting his head impatiently, he turned away to order another beer from the grubby bar-owner in his slovenly shirt, who looked as though he spent his days waiting behind the counter for the prices to rise and the tide to fall.

'Cerveza, Bier, birra, bière, beer,' Alexis called with a flourish − another echo of those old novels where knights enter the inn and bellow, 'Out of my way, varlets!' − but the man behind the counter merely pointed towards the big refrigerated chest.

'Do I have to go and get it myself?'

Alexis got up and rummaged through the cooler, and when he turned around again there was no sign of the Gypsy or her cards, or of Max and Irène, who must have been off somewhere paddling in the prehistoric mud of the bay.

So Irène couldn't make up her mind to love him. Instead, she kept telling him off. Or pretending to get along really well with Max. Too bad for her. Even as a Wanderer, Alexis would be divine with his moustache and beard parted into two beautifully smooth wings, raising the index finger on his right hand as the shepherds approached. Even as a Wanderer, he would be a Christ rising from the tomb.

'If we don't leave right now,' Alexis told Irène, 'we'll have to spend the night here.'

She sat down and brushed a few twigs off her T-shirt. 'Can I have some bread and cheese?'

'You didn't hear me,' Alexis said, holding the food out to her.

'I'm hungry.'

Before she took a bite, she added, 'I really feel like a truck.'

'Oh, give me a break,' Alexis said, 'I was joking.'

'No, no,' she said. 'There's nothing you can do about it.'

'I'm annoyed that I smashed the statuette.'

'Really?'

'What annoys me most, actually, is that you guys are making a big tragedy out of it.'

'We're not the ones making a tragedy out of it,' said Irène.

'So who is, then?'

'They are,' she said, looking gloomy.

And when he asked her to explain, she just carried on chewing her bread and cheese. But her chin was pointing towards the figurines standing rigid on the beach.

It was already getting dark when Max came back, carrying one of the statuettes under one arm, a woman wearing a one-piece bathing suit with big blue and red flowers on it. The paint on her cheeks was peeling off.

'She's got a bit sunburnt,' Max remarked, putting it down near Irène. 'Don't you think she's cute?'

'Cute, shoot, fruit,' Irène murmured. 'You want to take it with you?'

'I don't know,' he said.

'She'd make a nice quiet bride,' Alexis commented.

'We'll spend the night here,' announced Max. 'What I'd like would be to find some water so I can wash.'

'Do you know you look like the statue of the muscly guy on lifeguard duty?' Irène asked.

'I've always wanted to be a lifeguard,' Max answered, 'but they made me take economics.'

'Who's "they"?' Alexis asked.

Max started dancing, holding the clay bathing-beauty in his arms. He twirled about, singing, 'They, it's you, it's me, it's them, it makes your head spin.'

After eating nearly all their remaining food, they got up to go for a walk. Along the way they discovered more statuettes among the trees and gave them names according to who they thought they looked like: they gave rock-star Johnny Hallyday a friendly smack on the head and adjusted Jacques Chirac's glasses for him.

'Our souls,' said Irène, sounding disillusioned.

They started walking down a track. Irène gave one hand to Alexis, the other to Max, and they went forward beside the perfumed lavender fields, their future rising to meet them in shades of blue and violet, while the last bees headed back to their hives, the sun dipped behind the earth and the shadow of the brambles filled the derelict house. They walked along peaceably, scarcely speaking, and turned back only when the sky was drained of light and sprinkled with anaemic stars, and the countryside bathed in the ghostly confrontation between white stones and black bushes.

Leaning against the low wall, the five clay tourists were still smoking their dead cigarettes, and keeping their eyes fixed on the invisible beach. As they passed the crushed body of the Pauper, Alexis stepped on his glasses and grumbled that it was just his luck, but the others didn't know whether he was talking about the Pauper or himself. Then they lay down on their sleeping bags, far enough apart for each of them to have the whole sky and the forest to themselves.

It was this expression, to have the whole sky and the forest to yourself, that brought tears to Irène's eyes, and she wept silently. In the end she sat up to say good night to the figurines, bowing before each one and murmuring, 'Mis-Truck greets you.'

She quite liked this name. In the past she'd dreamed she was turning into a little Indian girl: kidnapped from the village where she was born, she was adopted by an Ohlone tribe in a primitive California where people lived on fish and what they could gather along the banks of the rivers running from the Sierra Nevada. But 'Mis-Truck' . . . could a guy like Alexis ever find the name at all beautiful?

After she greeted Georges, the working man with the vinyl bag, he muttered in a thick working-class accent, 'Now, don't be crying, missy, it won't do no good. Look at us, we ain't crying no more.'

'It's just that . . .'

'I know,' the old housewife spoke up. 'You don't want to have the whole sky to yourself. We know you'd rather see it with one other person at least.'

'One other at least, what d'you think you're saying there!' cried Georges.

'Shut up, Georges, it's just that she's frightened she'll turn out like me.'

'I don't want to get old,' Irène admitted.

The other statuettes surrounded her.

'You've got no choice,' said White Hat, 'you either get old or you die before then. Unless . . .'

'Unless what?' sniffled Irène.

'Unless you do what we do,' announced Prof, 'which is, you stay in-between, the dead on one side, the living on the other. Immortal, don't you know, like the members of the Académie française.'

Irène shook her head, even more despairing. That wasn't her idea of a choice at all.

'I don't want to. You're in, how can I put it, a terminal stage. But I don't want to be one thing or the other, anything definite, like a secretary or a housewife, or a company director. Or I could be, but not for too long, just long enough to play at it and get out.'

'Get out,' repeated a chorus of high and low voices.

'Play at it,' other voices went on.

'What about us, then?' growled Prof. 'Your friend the Risen Christ killed one of us. He crushed him, he'll have to take his place.'

'His name's Alexis, for starters,' Irène said, 'and he didn't do it to be mean.'

'Sorry, love,' Georges objected. 'Even if he done it from lack of class consciousness, he killed one of our comrades, we can't just let him leave.'

'Yeah,' shouted the housewife, suddenly furious, 'he's got to pay.'

'The Risen Christ stays,' Prof declared in a pompous voice. 'You and Pretty Beanpole, you can go off and turn into your own characters.'

'What do you mean, "Pretty Beanpole"? You mean Max? And here I thought you were happy to be yourselves.'

'We are happy!' they chorused.

'And then,' Irène continued, 'do you mean I'm going to wind up like you in the end?'

'At the very end, Big Truck,' Black T-shirt said gently. 'Not before that, and you don't know yet . . .'

'The less you know, the faster you end up like that,' the Belgian Guy announced.

'You mean I'm going to end up as Big Truck without noticing? That's horrible. I liked Mis-Truck. As long as I was mis-made I was nothing. Go away, go away quickly or I'll crush the lot of you.'

She was alone, looking at the sky between the bushes. Thin wisps of cloud trailed beneath the stars; there must be a wind blowing up there now. She thought about the boundless time-frames of the universe, the cycles of the rocks and the planets they'd been told about in school, and she shivered, thinking that something like infinity stretched before the statuettes. Of course, they were paying for it by living life in very slow motion, and they weren't safe from accidents. In fact, they were even more vulnerable than any animal, but their needs were so few, and they didn't feel anything any more except a little nostalgia and a very vague fear of being destroyed.

And now, on the pretext that he'd crushed the Pauper, Alexis was going to have to take the statue's place. But under what law, in the name of what justice had he sealed his fate? And all because he'd been afraid of a tarot card and a fortune-teller's dodgy reading.

Alexis was supposed to become a teacher in two years' time: that was the choice he'd made, maybe partly under pressure, but his choice all the same. One day he'd have kids too, and that look of Christ rising from the tomb would soon fade. He'd be teased about it so often that he'd keep it up for a year or two more at most. Then he'd cut his hair, get rid of his floaty shirts, and turn into someone else.

'You've got no right to keep him as the Risen Christ,' she shouted. 'Just be patient, he'll come to you in some other form, but he'll come to you in the end.'

'Oh, oh,' the figurines replied. 'But which of us got to choose what we are? Who wanted to weigh a hundred kilos, to go bald, get wrinkly, be stooped with age?'

'It's better than being a Barbie doll,' Irène declared, 'at least you've lived. You can't take Alexis away from me, we love each other.'

The word rang in her ears like a great cathedral bell amid their laughter. Isn't it true that love is what conquers everything in its path?

'Oh, oh,' the figurines said again, 'was it love that made the Risen Christ trample the character standing in his way?'

'But love isn't free,' Irène responded, shouting to make herself heard. 'It falls for an illusion, and without that illusion it would be lost, it would burst out all over the place.'

'It's *love* that's the illusion,' the figurines sang, now in a mocking circle.

Irène announced that she would make two statuettes the next day: one of a very good-looking boy, the other of a very good-looking girl – at least they'd be her idea of good-looking – and she would call that the end of love.

She felt her heart beating very hard: she would do it.

She stood up, hunched over, felt the strength in her thighs and shoulders, rolled herself into a ball and began to purr, softly at first, like a cat, then as loudly as an engine. She stepped on the gas, made her eyes shine brightly, rubbed her breasts until they lit up the way, started off with a jolt, ran over a sharp stone that made her groan, pushed the first figurine, Black T-shirt, out of the way, then one of an actor she didn't have time to recognise. Zigzagging drunkenly, she swerved around the bush where the housewife stood shouting at her, 'You reckless driver! You killer!' while Georges yelled, 'Help, help!' Now Alexis would be able to leave, Big Truck had done the hard work for him.

LIFE IN CHAPTER IV

Now that it's finished, I think I understand. But in fact, all I'm doing is seeing her over and over again. I see her coming into the room where there are still two students hanging around; then off they go, and there I am with chalk on my fingers even though I haven't touched the chalk. She's just as lovely as the year before, maybe even lovelier because I wasn't expecting to see her again. She looks like one of Van der Weyden's Virgins; it's her red hair, perhaps, or the way she holds herself. Her name comes back to me straight away, Louise, and she's holding a big manila envelope: a friend's manuscript. She didn't say *my* friend, I noticed particularly. 'Just the first three chapters,' she says, 'because he hasn't managed to write any more than that.'

I would rather talk about her, but she just repeats that the writer couldn't get any further with his novel, she shakes her head, shrugs, and I take the envelope. I'm not sure what she wants from me, but I'll at least phone her. 'There it is,' she says, pointing at the number written below the title in red ink, *The Saviour.* 'An evangelical piece?' I ask, teasingly. She looks down, and that's when I notice the dark circles under her eyes, her crooked smile, and again that hair I'd love to thrust my hands into.

I start reading as soon as I get back to my hotel room.

It's the story of a young Belgian man of Sicilian origin – which explains his name, Salvatore – who goes through a spiritual crisis. His life has lost all meaning, his relationships have lost their spice, his family has become deeply disappointing to him. He decides to go on a retreat in a monastery, something he's got interested in from reading pseudo-gothic novels, among them *The Name of the Rose.* He talks about it to a priest he's known since he was a boy, and the priest finds a retreat for him in a Capuchin priory near Parma. He goes there and is soon on friendly terms with some of the brothers, whose names are Francesco, Leonardo and Médard. After he's been there for five days at most, he realises that the so-called friendship of these brothers is a cover for the crassest of sexual appetites. Salvatore is described as a sweet innocent who is invited one evening to visit the crypt of the priory, where he's ambushed, nearly gets himself raped, and manages to defend his chastity only by the vigorous use of his fists. Bruised, confused, he seeks shelter in the office of the prior, a holy man who, alas, after listening to Salvatore's complaint, exposes himself in the most vile manner. Poor Salvatore leaps out of the window and runs off into the night, through the countryside, with no money, no papers, practically no clothes. Not without difficulty, he manages to get himself back to Brussels. End of Chapter I.

Chapter II opens with a letter addressed to a Belgian bishop, in which Salvatore denounces the dreadful misconduct of the Capuchins. Next we see Salvatore going back to his normal life, taking a job as a van driver and being visited by the priest who brings him the bishop's reply: Salvatore must look within himself to find the reason for these serious accusations. The church inquiry has in fact found that they are baseless. Well, then I must be mad! cries the desperate Salvatore. And he opens his heart to his new girlfriend, a young redhead with a striking resemblance to one of Van der Weyden's Virgins. Scandalised by his revelations, she's supportive, and sorry for him. Some time later, Salvatore feels depressed once again and wants to get away from Brussels. He writes to a Scottish monastery, asking to go on a retreat. He manages to get himself there (partly thanks to the money his red-headed girlfriend lends him) and is taken in by Cistercian monks. At first he finds blissful peace at the monastery. In a letter he talks about the existence of divine sensual pleasure within the realm of man. One of the monks, Brother John, becomes his particular friend, and the profundity of their conversations shows Salvatore what chaos his life has been up till now. But one evening, after Salvatore goes down to the crypt with Brother John, they're joined by two other silent monks, and their prayers turn into a priapic orgy. The perverts jump on poor

Salvatore, who once again is saved only by the strength of his arms. The next scene is rather reminiscent of some of Sylvester Stallone's films. After triumphing over the three lubricious demons, leaving them lying battered on the floor, Salvatore spends the night hiding under a trailer and escapes the next morning in the garbage truck. After long and arduous travels he manages to return to Brussels.

In Chapter III, Salvatore learns that back in the United Kingdom the Cistercian monastery has laid a complaint against him for assault, and he lets his girlfriend know at great length just how offensive he finds this. So he writes to the Pope to denounce the vice and corruption to which he has been exposed. While awaiting an answer, he finds work as a bank teller. But he quickly falls into depression again, and with the help of a French priest he manages to go on another retreat in an abbey near Dijon. Alas, he discovers that the brothers are sodomites who try to rape him, and he escapes this terrible fate only because of his heroic resistance, in a brawl in which he flattens several of his attackers. He runs off into the night, goes back to Brussels, but he knows that more complaints will be laid against him. The world is closing in around him. Where can he hide?

Nowhere! I told myself, putting down the final page. How could he go on without killing himself or someone else? At first I lay down on my bed, but something in my reading had made me feel uneasy. I opened the window, the noise of the cars rose up towards me, a few pigeons flew off, and I looked out over the roofs, thinking to myself: out there, they're out there. This story was autobiographical: that's why it was repetitive. Otherwise, the repetition would have been a deliberate choice and that critical distance between the writer and his text would have allowed the story to come to a conclusion. It was my job to know these things, it was part of what I taught, and Louise knew this. Louise who, it was obvious, was the lovely student in the story and therefore the author's mistress. Mistress of pseudo-Salvatore. Things couldn't have been all that great between them.

No, and that was why she'd come to me for help.

I dialled the number, and she picked up the phone straight away. Her voice sounded breathless, as if she'd run. 'Oh no,' she said, 'I didn't run, I don't know . . .' She stopped, and her panting into the receiver was sending me unbearable vibrations, making the hair on the back of my neck stand up. I started to babble: 'It's a fascinating piece, but it's repetitive, although of course repetition can be very good sometimes . . . Take Ravel's *Bolero,* for example.'

She couldn't follow me, I was talking past her or over her, talking mechanically.

'Are you OK?' I blurted out. 'Are you OK?' I was dying to show her that I knew, that it was totally obvious: this guy, her boyfriend, Salvatore's creator, Salvatore himself . . .

'No,' she answered all of a sudden.

'No what?'

'I'm not OK, not OK at all.'

'Is it him?' I asked, lowering my voice. 'He's jealous, is that it?'

Suddenly I was convinced that he beat her. Maybe even because of the manuscript she'd brought me. I thought of one of my friends who'd lived with a stone-cutter for a year, admiring his powerful arms and his simplicity right up until he started to beat her. In the end, he wouldn't let her leave the house. She would crouch in the corner of the shower when he came home. The neighbours, the cops, everyone thought she was crazy.

'Is he like he is in the story?'

'Come over,' she said, faintly. 'Please, won't you come over?'

Hearing this call for help, this pleading, I was practically beside myself. Then I heard something like a sob. A noise, it sounded like furniture being moved, books falling.

'Please come,' she repeated in a muffled voice.

'I'm on my way. What's the address, what address?'

But she'd already hung up. Or perhaps he had. And then I realised that I did have the address, in Louise's handwriting. No more excuses. Her boyfriend could actually turn into a killer, I thought. Yes, murder was a possible and logical conclusion to this story. And I was going to stick my nose in, to rescue someone. But what if it was me he killed? What if they made up and got back together again over my dead body?

I went out without having reached a decision. All my thoughts were contradicting one another. And yet I was moving on, or rather I was on the move: my feet were taking me towards the taxi stand although I thought I was caught up in the crowd of tourists heading towards Grand-Sablon square. I got into a car without really paying attention. But as soon as I got in everything changed: I was on a mission, I was the saviour, I was taking over the controls. Louise had called on me twice in the same day to sort out this story that wasn't going to limit itself to the paper version. To hell with narrative distance! To hell with Salvatore, he'd only be getting what he'd been asking for. I'd save his story for him – I was holding it in my hand, the envelope rolled into a stick – and for my trouble I'd get Louise.

The taxi had roared away along with my new resolution and was charging through the darkness. Lights were starting to glow in the windows, like the fiery tips of the cigarettes I was longing for. It was my desire that was propelling the taxi along. The driver had sensed it, he was laughing, showing huge white teeth between his dark lips. 'Go on, open it,' he said when I wound the window down, 'Nice, nice,' waving grandly towards the sky. As he accelerated he barked out clumsy statements, finishing them off by stamping on the brakes, sending me crashing into the front seat. He played his cab like an organ: even the chassis squealed as he took the corners. And I was laughing too, by the open window, because of the wind blowing into my mouth, smoothing back my hair, and thinking about

Louise. And then he suddenly slowed down, looking anxiously all around. He needed a piss, it had been niggling at him for ages and now he just couldn't wait any longer. Instead of heading straight for our street, he started looking for a likely spot, and when I protested, 'But it's an emergency, a woman may be dying', he answered, 'Gotta pee, gotta pee', pulling terrible faces, grabbing his crotch obscenely. He was driving really slowly, one hand on his fly and the other on the steering wheel, peering into dark corners. 'Over there,' I told him, 'over there', pointing towards a bar. But he didn't want to pay for a beer which would have made him pee even more an hour later. And my Louise was still waiting, must still have been waiting when he stopped behind a building site hidden in darkness, when he went off, with the car keys but leaving the lights on for me. I slumped down on the back seat, everything seemed to be losing focus, floating away on a tide of inessential, anecdotal, everyday details. With all the turning this way and that, Brussels had become immense, we were stuck indefinitely in parts of the city I'd never seen, and when we finally came to a screeching halt in front of the house I asked, 'Is this it? What time is it?' unable to extricate myself from my seat.

And then it was night, a dark building, names on a badly lit plaque. I rang. Nobody answered. I rang again, I waited, I went to the phone booth on the corner. Still nobody. I started to check out the dark mass of the building, counting the windows that were showing a light, wondering which one was Louise's, feeling more and more sober as I counted and stayed on the footpath opposite, trying to look cool and calm, without even a cigarette. Obviously I was an idiot, because people who aren't idiots don't find themselves in such a jam. A few minutes later the door opened to let out a couple of lovers, but I didn't know the girl. I rushed into the entrance, I went up to their floor, I knocked at their door, I waited, I listened intently – not a sound from inside – I hammered on the door, nobody ever opened it.

I shoved the manuscript under the door, crushing it and tearing it practically in half, and then I left. I've heard nothing since.

Whenever I talked about the travels of Salvatore I left out this part of the story: I just talked about the three monasteries. There was one particular evening, about eighteen months later, in the Touraine region, when I made a group of friends laugh again with the story of Salvatore's trials and tribulations, and we drank a merry toast to his adventures. The next morning one of the group, an American, told me something else. When he was in Berkeley, in August, he'd been invited to a wedding. The bride was a gifted student, ravishingly beautiful and full of energy, from a socially prominent family – in a word, a dream. And the man she was going to marry clearly wasn't fit to tie her shoelaces. He was Belgian, young, highly strung, and he talked too fast in bad English; he'd come to Berkeley to study theology. He had intended to become a priest, but he'd changed his mind when he fell in love with this gorgeous Californian. Although she came from a well-known protestant family, the young woman had agreed to convert and the wedding was to take place in a Catholic church.

'We were waiting,' my American friend explained, 'and the groom was late. The church was completely full, family, friends, everyone was getting quietly impatient, and I could hear whispered jokes about men who can't make up their minds. And then after half an hour the priest stepped forward. In a voice so quiet and low that we had to listen really hard, he announced that the marriage would not take place because the bridegroom didn't feel ready to make his vows. "Let us pray," he said, clasping his hands against his chest and bending his head. A crushing silence answered him. The bride seemed to stagger, and her father held her so she didn't fall. Because she was immediately surrounded I couldn't see her face. As the noise level started to rise and people began to leave, the father called for silence. His daughter, pushing back her veil, spoke out in a voice that seemed drained of all its strength but still resonated through the whole church: "Dear friends, we had prepared a reception in the Botanic Gardens. It wasn't just for me, but for you as well, and I invite you all to come along. I will be there myself." If her fiancé heard this voice he'll be aware for the rest of his life what he's missing.'

The American shook his head in disbelief.

'Yes,' I said, 'Salvatore.'

'Oh, Salvatore?' he responded, suddenly amused. *'Salvator?'* I laughed with him, but sourly. I had a feeling of oppression in my chest and a bizarre urgency. I really had to talk to Louise, I really had to tell her.

I had trouble getting her new phone number, and as soon as she heard me speak, her voice sank. As if she were hiding. But she wasn't hostile. And I said, triumphantly, 'I've found Chapter IV.'

She listened to me, laughing, understanding what I was talking about even when I went on about the cross-over between writing and life. I was so happy she was in good spirits that I kept showing off my intellect. But I was burning to ask her where she went to that evening when I knocked at her door. And couldn't I go back? Take her dancing somewhere? Cheek to cheek? Instead of which I said, 'How's Salvatore?'

Again that hesitation, then in a neutral voice she explained that he had left her. Not to go to California, but to hide away in Sicily, where in the most traditional way imaginable he'd married a woman whose dialect he could barely understand. It was as if he led a cloistered existence. He didn't write to his family in Belgium any more and didn't answer personal letters.

So was this how his novel had ended?

I was listening to Louise's breathing in the receiver. That panting, hunted way she breathed.

She was with someone else.

'Does he beat you?' I murmured.

There was a silence that hurt my ears, and in the middle of it Louise swallowed noisily.

'Repetition . . .' I blurted.

But she hung up so quietly I didn't hear the click.

HERE'S TO GOOD BEER

One life, one, only one, and in that life thousands of others like drops of beer splashing out when you set your glass down again. When you smack it back down on the counter. Then Stan licks his lips with his thick tongue, his wide-stretched, almost flabby lips. That's Stan, and I'm watching him out of the corner of my eye.

The waiter is wearing a fixed smile. 'Happy hour,' he says. 'Two for the price of one!' And he refills our glasses, letting the head run down the sides.

Stan had explained to me on the phone that he wanted to talk to me, no reason, just to get to know me, after that other time, when he'd played at Vincent's, where there's that one-eyed cat, the one-eyed cat at the Porte d'Orléans. He'd added, 'Meet me at the Buffon, it's dark outside, I won't be able to make out the numbers on the buildings.'

He must have been at the bar for a while, sitting on a stool and drinking while he waited for me. His amplifier is leaning against the wall, with a grey cover over it. Only the wheels are sticking out, it's handier for dragging it through the Metro where Stan sings mushy English folk-songs. At his age! Old, sweaty, short of breath, in the Metro! Yes, and now he's all swollen up with the beer. He's rolling his eyes, even rounder behind the thick glasses. It's a sweet kind of roundness, reminds me of kids' marbles veined with lots of different colours. And there's a film of sweat on his skin reflecting blurry objects, the glow of the lights, the waiter's shadow. In the folds lurks the fatigue of the day, deep and colourless. He turns his head slowly towards me and says, 'That's why I phoned. After what Vincent told me I wanted to get to know you – your inner man.'

He's talking, and his words are falling over everything like a blanket, like snow, probably because his accent makes them all somehow the same. He's telling me about a night, a long time ago, when he picked up two hitch-hikers in the South of France, and a concert he went to with them, in a field, under the stars. It was so magical that he must have got stuck on it, because when he goes to take a piss and comes back, he starts telling the same story again. He wipes his forehead, and by way of conclusion he says, 'I'd like to get to know your inner man.' Looks to me like some sort of tic he's got.

We walked back up the boulevard. I was pulling his amplifier along, and he was rolling along in the light from the last shop windows, a massive man, lurching to the left then getting his balance before lurching off to the right, like a barrel. And when I noticed that he didn't have a guitar, I told myself that perhaps it wasn't just an amplifier I was dragging, but a complete sound-system where he could play a cassette and pretend to be singing as he held out his hand for money.

Pretend to be singing as he held out his hand!

When we got to my place we carried on drinking, Jenlain beer, and he swore he was going to give me a really valuable gift, show me something I wouldn't find anywhere else, a way of writing. He started by rolling himself a joint, slowly, wetting the paper thoroughly and putting in plenty of weed. He kept on saying, 'You must have seen this before, with artists.'

He raised one thick eyebrow, then the other.

We each took a piece of paper and drew up a column: A B C D E F . . .

'Let's start with A,' he said.

I announced 'apple', and wrote it down on my quarter-page. He nodded and with a knowing smile, said, 'That's sexual.' As for him, he'd written 'absolute'.

For B, I put 'bomb', and he repeated, 'That's sexual.' He wrote 'beer'.

For C, I wrote 'cat'.

'As in "pussy",' I said. Stan twisted his neck to read my page, but this time he didn't say anything.

He was sweating more and more heavily. His belly looked to me as heavy and dense as a sack of cement. Suddenly he started talking about chess: in his great generosity, he was going to teach me how to play that, too, because it's a game that's bigger than all the world. He rubbed his forehead and added, 'In the world, you see, you can't lose yourself to the same degree, because there's always hunger to guide you.'

I felt as if there was less and less light in the room, and that what little there was of it was shining on our hands and our pieces of paper.

We were up to H. I said, 'Hiccup.' He said, 'Hagebra', and I made him repeat it. He opened his mouth wide, 'Ha-ge-bra.' With a big puff of air for the *h* and rolling the *r* as he lifted his eyes to the ceiling. I said OK.

For N, I wrote down 'Noah'. His word was 'ninny'. Then he said: 'Let's stop there, otherwise we'll have too many words to make a text. Nothing stifles a text quicker than words.'

But he was the one being stifled. His Adam's apple looked out of true. It settled down when he threw his head back and started laughing like a little kid, with a cheerful round face and dimples in his cheeks. Then his heavy, dense head came back to face me, with its thick glasses, its wrinkled forehead, and especially its teeth. When he opened the dark hole of his mouth I could see them, brown, green, red, a whole landscape razed by a chainsaw, bits of macaroni sliced off level with his gums.

He let his voice rise: a groaning sound to start with, then it turned into singing for a few seconds. A snatch of a very sweet melody that pulled all that mass of flesh upwards. His lips in a big O. Wrinkles on his forehead and cheeks, I couldn't tear my eyes away from them: I could read a whole life engraved there, but it would have taken another lifetime to decipher it. And the joint he'd shoved into the corner of his mouth, vibrating with the beginnings of his song. He stopped, breathed in with a bubbling sound, and started to talk about his text again, about *the habsolute hagebra that lays in white for the egoist.*

I drained what was left in my glass. 'That whole sex thing,' I said, 'it's a dream . . . the fields in summer, the concert under the stars and all that . . . all that . . .'

He giggled.

So I went on in a neutral voice, 'Let's talk about "London" for "L" and "son" for "S".'

His eyes revolved in all directions. I'd pushed his button, the one that won't turn off once it's turned on. 'I know that's painful,' I said with a hypocritical smile.

He closed his eyes.

'So what about that text?' he grunted after a bit.

There was a moment's silence. He was stuck on 'son'.

'Doesn't want to see me any more,' Stan blurted out. 'He refuses to see his father. His father!'

He spat out the last word like a loose tooth. His head fell forward. He huddled into the armchair, tapped at the ashtray with one finger, then, after dragging on his joint, he launched into a muddled story where his son accused him, him, Stan, of abandoning him when he left his job to devote himself to music. But it wasn't true, it was all a dirty trick played by his ex-wife, his brother, his parents, his parents-in-law, his uncles, his aunts – no one would have suspected that he had such a large family and that they were all, every last one of them, in league against him.

In the silence that followed, each of us breathed in echo of the other. Heavy breathing, heavy eyelids.

'It's just another story,' Stan concluded. 'Happens all the time.'

I smiled. For a chess player, that was weak. Very weak. It was hard not to go for the checkmate straight away, by replying nastily, as his evasiveness deserved, with an 'It's your life' spoken gently and definitively.

All I said was, 'I didn't know *men* had to choose between art and motherhood as well . . . or in your case, fatherhood.'

Silence.

I persisted, 'I thought that was a woman's problem.'

He shook his head.

I felt he was so undeveloped, so very undeveloped, so squishy actually, that it made me want to dig my hand delicately into the rolls of fat on his belly or even into the big hole in his face. I was mad at him for being fat, for going into the Metro, for being poor. I was turning into his family, his son who didn't want to hear another word about him any more, his brother who'd never been able to stand him. I got up.

'Want another Jenlain?'

While I was getting the beer out of the fridge, he went to take another piss.

We bent over our pages again. I wasn't following too well any more. Words, bits of life, so to speak, like in dictionaries — the whole universe through the alphabet. It seemed ludicrous to me. Of course, 'house, Noah, son, water, frail, island' and so on, each one of them could be a story, a book, a life. But Stan took my piece of paper and put his finger on it. 'At random,' he grunted, and then, reading out what was under his index finger, 'Night.'

'That's not one of my words,' I said.

'Of course it is.'

'No, I wrote "Noah".'

I looked at the place he was showing me on the page; it was dirty, almost impossible to make out.

'You've smudged it with your sweaty finger,' I said. 'Yeah, your sweaty finger. What I wrote was "Noah".'

'No, not Noah, "night", black as night.'

'It's not "night". At best, it's unreadable.'

We were going to have a drunkards' quarrel. I could tell from the way we were breathing that something was brewing blindly, an urge to fight. Something that not even our tiredness would calm.

'It's clear, it's clear, it's clear,' he insisted.

The clearest thing I could see on the paper was Stan's thumbprint and the ink that had run from his sweat. A stain, a grubby mark. And that's what he would have used to gamble on my destiny?

'Clear as night, clear as the black cat,' I said.

'Hey hey', said Stan, leaning forward. 'Well, excuse *me*.' And he belched. It was so loud I imagined I could smell it.

I repeated, 'The black cat.'

Stan looked at me, his right eye closed, as if to say 'My

eye', and his expression changed to one of satisfaction, very irritating. 'The cat?' he asked. 'The one-eyed cat at Porte d'Orléans?' He was cocky, taking the mickey, and I couldn't see why. There was a kind of coating over the top of us, making things incomprehensible, making words thick and slippery.

'It ain't one-eyed,' I said. 'That cat is deaf. It's the *deaf* cat at Porte d'Orléans. D'you hear me, Stan? D'you hear me?'

'No kidding.' His eyes were rolling again.

I stood up. 'No kidding, eh, no kidding.'

There was a strange smell coming from him, not exactly unpleasant, but pickled, and I held my nose. I could feel myself swaying. He stood up, too, with so much difficulty that I felt he must crack.

And he said, 'You want to kill me, you do.'

I shook my head, as if I couldn't take any more. But it was true that at one point I'd thought about what they used to do in the country in the old days to kill the mice that came to eat the wheat. They put a bit of plaster in with the flour, and when the mice were good and full they would drink. And the plaster would set, blocking their intestines. Yes, I'd thought about that when I looked at Stan's big belly.

'No,' I said, 'why would I want to kill you?'

Stan shook his head, did an about-face and went on his way. Out on the landing, he turned and repeated his refrain: 'I wanted to get to know your inner man.'

He swallowed and added, 'I saw nothing.'

'You didn't see anything,' I replied sulkily.

'No, I didn't not see anything. I saw *nothing.*'

At that he flushed purple.

I helped him get his amplifier downstairs. He set off slowly along the street, the wheels on his equipment clanking as he went. It made me think of an invalid in a wheelchair. And in the distance, at the far end of the interminable boulevards, there was a halo over the rooftops, as if all the light was gathering together into a faint glow, a sort of low-level cancer, the silent spread of people unable either to stay awake or to sleep, to live or to die.

At home I had good lighting, as unfailing as in a prison. Darkness was reduced to a fringe of shadow behind objects and edging the pools of light. Here, at the foot of the lamp-post, the dark traced out its lacy border, almost warm, a kind of protection. An enlightened darkness, you might say, something comfortable. Nothing to do with the 'night' and the 'nothing' that Stan had tried to fob off on me like counterfeit money. Not to mention his claim that he'd got to know my 'inner man'. Yeah, well, you bit off more than you could chew with my inner man, and you won't be getting another taste of him for a while, that's for sure! And teaching me to write. And the one-eyed cat. It's not one-eyed, it's deaf. Yes, I'm sure of that, and if need be I'll check it out tomorrow, and I'll find out if it's deaf like Stan or one-eyed like me. I'll get things sorted. Just like before, minus the bits of paper, of course. It's impossible to glue them together again and get back to the blank page, the page before his disgusting finger and his words that were supposed to make every possible kind of story, but in actual fact it was always the same one, always just as pathetic. We can't cover up the tear, that tiny fringe of fibres that runs along the edge of the paper. Stan was wrong when he said I wanted to kill him. No, what I wanted was much more radical, more absurd. I wanted him never to have existed, like a brother that fate (not your parents, they're far too weak to have wanted this child) has inflicted on you and that you'll be stuck with for ever. Stuck like the shadow that sprouts from our feet and that we still never manage to walk on.

THE LITTLE SHOP OF HOPE

for Françoise Wuilmart

I was happy at my work, feverishly finishing off my translation of an essay on suicide. In three days I'd have finished (I was at the revision stage), I'd jump into my car and take off towards the south – Namur, Metz, Lyon – en route for a holiday during the quiet part of August. In Nîmes I would give my translation to the publisher (he'd forgive me for being a month late, I hear he likes me, he says, 'Pauline, she's a great translator'), and from there I'd take off again for Montpellier, Barcelona and . . .

And that bastard just beneath my window, clacking away with his shears for the last hour and more. His hedge-clippers. A clack–clack that was sometimes crisp and final (thank goodness!), sometimes fussy, grating, endless, unbearable.

As unbearable as the neighbour himself. But I wasn't about to let that ridiculous man ruin my morning's work – on such a radiant morning, with the sky a clear blue after two days of rain. I thumped my pile of papers down onto the desk and went over to the window. He was just below me, perched on a stepladder, struggling to cut the top of the hedge evenly. In my mind I shouted out his name: Hardel! Henri Hardel! Stripped to the waist (hairless bony chest, white flabby skin), a fag in his mouth, long skinny arms, he was working away with his clippers, and the leaves of the cherry laurel hedge were falling like hair around a hairdresser's chair. The top of his skull, deep red in the sun, was as shiny as some creature's shell. A great big lobster adapted to life in a garden.

Suddenly I felt sorry for him. Maybe because of all his effort, his jutting shoulder blades, the cigarette that distorted his face. He was an exceptionally ugly man (he looked like Mr Potato Head, yes, that was it, with his big lumpy nose and sparse red hair), but he didn't look as if it caused him any grief. He would even have been proud of it, as he was of his other defects. He'd turned his 'irregular' features into scars of battle: he'd got them at the hands of three drunks, who beat him up and left him for dead on the edge of the Quai aux Briques where his father ran a restaurant – he was fourteen at the time.

The source of his suffering, I realised at that moment, was something else. Hardel's face puckered up around his cigarette as if he could never suck on it hard enough, as if he were *attached* to its smoke. For years and years, the cigarette had been smoking Hardel (Henri), all his butts, their ash, embers and smoke had been weaving a big noose for him.

Henri Hardel, you're a smoked ham. That's what I told myself. And I'd be wasting my time feeling sorry for some prick who keeps his wife shut away, a penny-pincher who refuses to spend money on electric hedge-clippers that would probably be noisier but so much faster, and wouldn't make that squeaking noise when they jam on the twigs, that screech that's so irritating it's almost human.

If ever someone was asking to be rebelled against, it was Hardel. But I wouldn't waste my breath telling his wife that. She would just look at me with her dead fish-eyes, the eyes of a skate as painted by Chardin or Ensor (only less moving), and ask me if I could give her a lift into town. Because catching the bus to La Hulpe and then the train from there, it's tiring, you know.

But Hardel isn't a totally charmless despot, he's even the source of my prettiest bracelet and a silver brooch set with an emerald. When the Hardels moved in three years ago, they insisted on inviting me over, and I was more than a little surprised to see that their home was chock-full of beautiful objects. Well, perhaps not all of them beautiful, but very expensive, ranging from pewter pots from the Middle Ages to Empire-style carriage clocks. Hardel explained that he was a retired goldsmith. He told me specially that everything on display in his home was insured against theft. Did he mean the stuff wasn't stolen? Because at the same time he claimed to be living on such a tiny pension that you had to wonder how he could maintain this house in the greenest part of Ohain, let alone fill it with precious things.

'But we keep costs down,' he declared, completely serious, 'we don't have a *phone*! What for, when there's a booth a hundred metres down the road?' In fact, I never saw him go near it. Only his wife, Sabine, uses the booth. Or, when she can't avoid it, she comes and uses my phone. She's the one who gave me my bracelet, to thank me. 'From Henri,' she made a point of telling me.

I leaned out of the window. 'Hey, hey!'

Hardel (Henri) stopped and looked up. He was panting and his mouth was half-open, but still with the cigarette in it. His ribs rose and fell crazily.

'Isn't it a bit too hot to be working so hard?'

He swallowed, and said, in a sort of croak, 'Ah, Pauline, you sound like my wife.'

I couldn't tell whether he was smiling or whether it was just the sun glinting on his teeth.

Like his wife! That'd be the day. Sabine was fifteen years younger than him, and had an iron constitution – she worked like a dog, did Sabine. She needed to be tough, to put up with what came her way. I would see her sometimes getting off the bus, loaded down with groceries and a backpack that made her look like a hunchback, and she'd charge down the road as if her dearest desire was to hurry back home to her master.

And then there were Saturdays. Hardel would back out his Cadillac, an ivory coupé from the sixties, a huge thing with fins like a hydroplane, and spend an hour fussing over it, washing and polishing it, not to mention retouching the whitewalls on the tyres. Once the car was spick and span, he drove Sabine to the supermarket. I imagine he stayed in the parking lot beside his beautiful Cadillac, smoking Belgas and combing his hair in the wing mirror. Because, maybe to highlight his ugliness, he's vain and keeps a comb in his back pocket. When they got home they would drink, get all boozed up, and argue. I'd hear them shouting, along these lines: (*Her*) Everyone hates you, if I left you, you'd die of loneliness. (*Him*) Go on, then, leave me, you'll wind up working the streets, except no one will want you. (*Her*) Drop dead! (*Him*) When I do drop dead, then you'll really be in trouble. Because I'm not going to leave you a cent. And I'm never going to marry you.

So I'd shut the window and tell myself it was just as well I'd got divorced before things reached that point. But the voices would start up again in the house next door, and I'd think I heard muffled blows. I would imagine Sabine with her long, sad, fishy face, her cheeks just asking to be slapped, and I ached for her. One day, Hardel told me, a glass of gin in his hand: 'We're only married *behind the church*.' Proud of himself, his witty remark. Well, hooray, I thought, hooray for you. I felt terribly embarrassed for Sabine, who was listening impassively. Wake up! How come you don't kill him off, this fake husband of yours? D'you think you'd be any worse off in prison?

★

I went back to my work table, my computer. The keys were starting to stick to my fingers. I was having a hard time concentrating on my text.

Clack clack!

That cretin is stopping me from thinking straight!

At ten past twelve – I know the time because of the little Casio clock on my desk – Sabine started to yap, 'Henri! Henri!' Then her voice suddenly changed: 'Pauline! Pauline!'

I ran to the window and saw her standing on the grass, looking up towards me. At her feet, her man lay on his back, legs wide apart. I could only see the grey of his trousers with their green stains, and the soles of his shoes pointing ridiculously skywards.

'He's passed out,' shouted Sabine. 'Call the emergency services.'

That took me all of ten seconds, but I thought that right now he must be sorry he'd saved money on the phone line, the old cheapskate. And still, even today, it was his wife who had to deal with the hassle.

I charged downstairs, going out onto the street because of the fence separating our two gardens. And Sabine, distraught, said, 'I don't know what happened, I came out to tell him lunch was ready, and he was already lying on the ground.'

Henri's profile stood out like a piece of porcelain against the carpet of cut leaves; his cigarette was lying couple of feet away on a clump of grass.

Sabine put her hand on his chest. 'He's not breathing,' she said, 'it must be a heart attack.' Her own chest was heaving fit for two. Her lips twitched nervously. I asked her, 'Do you know how to do mouth to mouth?'

She turned towards me, her eyes glazed. 'Mouth to mouth?'

'Yes, you blow air into his lungs.'

She kept staring at me, but when she understood that I wasn't going to do it for her, she made up her mind.

'Like this?' she said, taking Henri's face in her hands.

She turned it to the side, and I saw that his eyes were open, but unblinking. I held my breath, I could feel a lump in my throat. She slipped a finger between his teeth.

'Like this?' Sabine said again, kneeling over him. 'Like this?' She lowered her head towards his mouth.

'Yes, go ahead.' I felt completely limp.

She started blowing.

'That's it,' I told her, 'go for it. Yes, it's making his chest rise.'

She was stopping every ten seconds to spit, wipe her mouth and catch her breath. And then she picked up the rhythm. She was holding Henri's shoulders and shaking him like a doll she'd been trying to inflate. His head kept falling sideways, but she grabbed his hair and his ears and they were locked in combat again. A bird hopped along the hedge; suddenly it started to sing in sharp trills, heart-breaking, drunk with joy.

When the emergency services arrived with all their sirens screaming, and people leaped out onto the lawn,

Sabine didn't even get up. I was the one who explained the situation to them, and they tapped Sabine on the shoulder. 'Let us do that, Madame.'

The ambulance pulled to a tyre-screeching stop behind the emergency services vehicle. Three men in white coats spilled out, leaving the doors open. 'What's the problem?' shouted the driver, a tall dark man wearing tortoise-shell glasses.

I pointed to the emergency services guys crouched around Henri's protruding soles with the blades of grass still sticking to them. The crouching figures stood up and, after exchanging a few words, carried Henri over to the ambulance. Someone put an oxygen mask on him while someone else injected a liquid into his arm.

One of the white-coated men came over with his clipboard to get some information from Sabine.

'Is he going to make it?' she asked.

'Absolutely.' Then, inspired, he added, 'We're going to intubate him.'

'It's a heart attack, I'm sure of it,' Sabine said in a dull voice.

'Has he had one before?'

'Two.'

'Great,' the man said, writing it down.

The others busied themselves around the patient. More injections, cardiac massage, and still the mask covering his nose and mouth.

'So that's it, this time?' Sabine asked.

'What do you mean, that's it?' the ambulance officer asked, stopping his writing.

'He's going to die?'

'Oh no, not at all, he's not going to die.'

'He's already pulled this on me twice,' Sabine said, turning towards me. 'Twice he's died, and twice he's been resuscitated.'

She was blinking, somewhere between terror and admiration.

The emergency services left quietly. The ambulance people were busy for another five minutes, then, with siren wailing, they took off for the hospital. They'd taken my phone number, and it was me they called an hour later to confirm that he was definitely, finally dead. What did I want to do with the body?

'I'll let his wife know.'

Lying on her flowery-patterned couch, her eyes on the ceiling, she was muttering, 'Whatever will become of me?'

I thought of a whole heap of ways she'd be better off without her Henri, but I couldn't tell her about them.

She shook her head slowly. 'He did it on purpose. You don't know what he's like, you don't know what he's capable of.'

I sighed. I didn't dare leave.

'Come on, come home with me and phone the hospital,' I said.

She got up with difficulty, and once on her feet she looked even more limp, like a great sack emptied by her misfortune, her arms hanging, her heavy hands like raw meat.

'And then you need to tell his family and friends.'

But there was no family left. Sabine had a sister living in England who'd never met Hardel. On his side, there was a distant cousin and a niece he hadn't seen for years but had named his sole heir. 'Just to hurt me!' Sabine said. 'She's the one who's going to throw me out onto the street.'

In the afternoon she caught the bus to go and see Henri one last time at the hospital morgue. I settled down to my translation, but with great difficulty. The text was getting away from me, passages I had liked now seemed incomprehensible to me. I thought the author didn't discuss the *forms* of suicide enough – for example, cigarettes or the clack-clacking of clippers.

Around 7 pm, Sabine came knocking. She didn't ring the bell, like a stranger, she went around the house and knocked on the kitchen window. Shy little taps with long pauses in between. I went downstairs and, seeing her broad, pale face, her tousled auburn hair, and especially her sweet, expectant expression, I was seized with the urge to be mean to her. But I pulled myself together and asked her to come in. I offered her a glass of port.

'I have to get all the jewellery out of the house,' she announced gloomily. 'I have to get it out of the way before his niece arrives, and takes the house and everything. Can I leave it with you?'

'In the cellar,' I sighed, 'locked away in a suitcase.'

Her eyes were damp with gratitude. She kept talking to me about Henri. 'He didn't trust women at all. He thought if he kept them under lock and key they'd be faithful to him. No, he didn't even believe that: he wanted to punish them *in advance* for their unfaithfulness! That's why,' she went on, 'he wanted me to die at the same time as him. He's jealous, even now, today, when I saw him at the morgue, he's jealous. He wants me to join him.'

'Why did you let him walk all over you?'

'Me? I fought him. Oh, I really fought. As much as I could.'

There was a silence. She swallowed and said, 'You don't know Henri. He's immensely rich. He used to open his safety-deposit box in front of me, at the bank, and he'd tell me to look at all the diamonds and the gold I'd never have. It'll go to the government, or his niece, but I'll be out on the street.'

'Well, you're not there yet,' I answered.

I should have held my tongue, put the top back on the bottle of port, told her I was hungry, or tired, gone to bed. But Sabine was settled solidly in my armchair, and her fear horrified me. She was trembling, she reminded me of a snail that had just lost its shell.

'Where's his safety-deposit box?' I asked.

'At the main branch of the bank, on Rue Sainte-Catherine.'

'Well, then, go and empty it out and you can hide all of it in my cellar.'

She responded with a helpless smile. During his visits

to the vault she'd managed to pick up the combination: PIE. (Planning ahead for this stage, of course, planning ahead.) And then, last month, Henri had punished her: 'I know you've seen the code, so I'm going to change it.'

She stopped speaking and all I could hear was her heavy breathing, filling the room. I thought their story was vile. Their dirty fight was still going on even after death. I closed my eyes so as not to see her any more and, when I opened them again, I said, 'If that's how it is, we'll get that box open.'

She turned slowly towards me.

'What? The box?'

'Yes.'

I poured her some more port and said, 'I'll go to the bank tomorrow, on Rue Sainte-Catherine. Give me the key and every single idea you've had about the new combination.'

Half an hour later, I was back at work, and to my great surprise I was able to immerse myself in my revisions. I went to bed around midnight, less tired than the previous night.

We had to act fast, open the box before the lawyer found out about it and sent an Inland Revenue agent to empty it. On the dot of ten o'clock I phoned the bank and asked about renting a safety-deposit box. The woman who answered offered me an appointment on Monday. I was insistent: 'Look, it's very urgent, I've got some high-value stocks and bonds I need to store safely, and

I'll open an account as well!' I could feel her hesitating, then she said, 'Come straight away, then.'

I had just enough time to gather together some papers and drive quickly to the centre of Brussels. At the bank, the assistant manager seemed reassured when she saw that I was a civil servant with a good job at the Institute of Slavic Languages. But all through our interview she kept giving my big Adidas bag puzzled glances – I'd put a few files in there, along with a smaller bag I was planning to use to carry off Henri Hardel's loot. I was waiting for her to ask me if I played tennis. But she didn't. In the end, she went with me to the vault – a long, narrow, windowless room that you could get into only after you signed the register and they opened the gate. They have a record of everyone who goes in. They gave me box 12 and, glancing at the numbered plaques, I saw that I was almost directly across from number 35, Hardel's.

After she'd showed me how to set up my own personal combination of three numbers or letters, the assistant manager said goodbye. I closed and opened my box without any problem, and put the smaller bag and my files inside. Then I crossed the room (empty, apart from a man in his fifties wearing a white polo shirt, who was sorting papers in front of an open box) to stand in front of number 35. I put the key in the lock, then turned the dials to spell the word PIE. Nothing. I tried all the similar combinations, listening carefully the way I'd seen people do in films, trying hard to detect the places where the mechanism might seem to want to stop by itself. After a couple of dozen attempts, I decided not to stay any longer. I didn't want to draw attention to myself, and besides I preferred to do some more research on Henri Hardel, because I knew that people don't choose their code at random. PIE must have had a meaning for him. My last attempt had therefore been 314. But, if Hardel was interested in figures, he'd hated school all the same and must have had unhappy memories of π. Too bad, I'd come back the next day, better prepared. I passed the assistant manager on the ground floor and I could tell, when she smiled at me, that she was still a little suspicious.

As soon as I was outside, dazzled by the sunlight, I shivered. Why, at the very moment when I was finishing my translation, had I got myself involved in such a crazy affair? Where are you going with this? I asked myself angrily. To prison? And then I got back into my Golf, started the engine and left my doubts behind me.

There were so many numbers, from Henri's weight, his waist measurement, his birth date, the address where he lived as a child, I'd filled columns with them. I was writing down names as well, and pretty soon I had a forest of letters in front of me that I couldn't make anything of. Unless I just dug around in there at random . . .

Sabine seemed as overwhelmed by events as usual, and she was getting on my nerves a bit more than the day before. I was starting to see what it was about her that had exasperated Henri Hardel. She had a hard time with the simplest tasks. For our research, the best she could do was go through old diaries and account books where Henri had written all kinds of things: numbers, of course, but completely trivial ones (purchase and sale prices, addresses, dates of meetings, phone numbers), and the occasional enigmatic sentence, like 'Spring has come, I know because I've had a letter from R.B.' And every time I asked Sabine a question about the meaning of these finds, she sat there in silence with that skate-à-la-Chardin expression on her face.

'Close those books,' I said in the end, a bit sharply, 'and look at me.'

Her mouth trembled slightly, and I wondered if she'd been drinking before I arrived. But suddenly, with a huge effort, she managed to get out: 'He preferred even numbers.'

'Ah, finally something useful!'

She added that he did it to get away from his attraction to the numbers 7 and 13, something he considered a superstition.

'Great. Did he have a lucky number?'

'Yes.'

'What was it?'

'Thirty-two.'

'So why didn't you tell me that?'

Her mouth started trembling again.

'So, why 32?'

The number was so important because when Henri was 32 he met the woman he called his great love.

'He wasn't shy about saying to me, "She's the only woman who could have changed my life, and she didn't want to." That hurt me like hell,' Sabine continued. 'It didn't make any difference that I told him over and over that it was just a delusion, a young man's dream, he wouldn't let it go. He played 32 at the races, or in the lottery, or else it was 3, 2 and 5, because that's 3 plus 2.'

'Did he win, with 32?'

'Not a thing. Which just goes to show he was only in love with himself, doesn't it?'

'What do you mean?'

'Because 32 was *his* age when he met that woman.'

I made do with the faintest of smiles. And then I asked, 'What was this woman's name?'

'Rachel Braun.'

I wrote down R.B.

'And he kept writing to her until she died in a car accident.'

'What year?'

'In 1991.'

I wrote down 11, then 9 and 1. Again, I was starting to have a lot of numbers. And in the silence that followed: 'Do you think he's with her now?' Sabine asked.

'Who, that woman? Now he's dead? You're joking. Didn't you say yourself he was just deluding himself?'

I was afraid I might start shouting.

When we tried to work out the meaning of PIE, Sabine explained rather slowly that it was the nickname of Henri's brother, short for magpie, because he always wore black and white when he performed. He sang and played the piano in cabarets.

'Is this brother the father of the girl who'll inherit everything?'

She nodded, yes.

That's when I realised that I'd stopped being exasperated a little while ago, now I was just sad and demoralised. I felt sorry for Sabine as I saw that all the people she'd tried so hard to get close to had never accepted her. There was nothing about her in Henri's notebooks and accounts. And even the word PIE, according to what she'd told me, was more closely connected to the hated niece than to her. Sabine must have been aware of this too. Because the more we fossicked about in the murky depths of the past, the more she hunched herself into the sofa. And she kept asking me at shorter and shorter intervals, 'Is that enough, now? Have you got everything?'

I could hardly tell her that if we carried on until we had everything she would die of disgust. So I stopped. 'We'll try with this,' I said.

She got up, and with slow, methodical movements, as if she was thinking them through, she piled up Henri's diaries and account books by the door. 'I'll find a box for them,' she said. Turning towards me, she added, 'I feel as though we've just buried him. It was easier with two of us.'

★

The next morning, in the vault, I tried various combinations of three letters, including the R for Rachel. But nothing worked. I have to admit that I was working feverishly, and that it was hard to concentrate. I felt discouraged. Our whole session the day before had apparently been for nothing. And that's when I started to think that PIE was me, the thieving magpie. Even though I was only trying to make sure justice was done. A really negative, defeatist idea, and I tried to get it out of my head but couldn't. That evening, I admitted to Sabine that I couldn't see how to open the box. Unless we called in professionals, who in our case would have to be burglars. All the more so since the funeral was to take place in two days' time – on Monday afternoon – and the bank would be notified of the death.

She listened to me, then, 'Pity,' she said slowly, 'pity.'

There was no blame in her voice, no bitterness. And for the first time we hugged each other.

Early on Sunday I packed my bags and put them in the boot of the Golf along with my translation. After Nîmes, I was planning to spend a week on the Costa del Sol with some Spanish friends. I was terribly pale: I'd get some sun and forget about Brussels. When I got back, Sabine would be in an entirely different situation.

As soon as I hit the motorway, I felt a great weight lifting off me and I started to drive very fast, too fast, even. It was as if the empty blueness of the sky and its bright little clouds were sucking me towards them, pulling me away from this suburb, this city, this life. I kept changing radio stations looking for music I liked, and I stopped at one playing Cuban songs that reminded me of films from my childhood, a time when my life was full of energy, when I went full steam ahead without knowing where I was going . . .

Huérfano soy en la vida, the singer lamented. Tomorrow, after my visit to the publisher, I would stop off at Irène's in Montpellier. Irène and her friend Giorgos, Greek, younger than her. When she showed me his photo she told me he had the most beautiful male organ she'd ever seen. But in the photo he was wearing clothes.

Yo no tengo padre, yo no tengo madre . . . I tried hard not to think about my father, who had died the previous year. My father used to say all the time, 'You *have to* live and you *cannot* live.' His second wife was very rich, as horribly greedy as Henri Hardel's. (I was fourteen when he remarried, fourteen.) When my father invited me for Christmas dinner, that woman made him pay for my share. She owned over 160 apartments in Brussels. She had masses of diamonds, but when she died there was nothing for me, not even the tiniest little bracelet. My father, sheepish, betrayed, admitted to me, 'I would have liked you to have some jewellery.'

I retorted, 'I wouldn't have wanted a single thing!'

Except that when I thought about it again now I felt like crying, and running away, tearing down this smooth, rolling motorway, exchanging the heavy fat north for the dryness of the south, freeing myself, moving back towards the centre of the earth where everything was weightless. And the further I went, the more upset I became.

Just before Langres I stopped for petrol. Because I'd been driving with the windows half-down, I felt groggy from the noise. The petrol station was flooded with sunshine, and the holiday-makers, with their shorts, their dogs, their bottles of water and their languid movements, looked like something out of a film. I could only follow them at a distance, not touch them or speak to them. I had a painful, disturbing feeling that I was becoming invisible, that I didn't really exist any more. I got a coffee from the machine and drank it, looking at the patches of sunlight on the concrete, the glittering cars, the teenagers who'd never seen a baseball game but were wearing baseball caps. It could have been anywhere. It was anywhere. Then I threw away my plastic cup and, when I found myself blinking in front of my dusty Golf, I realised that I was going the wrong way, I was going deeper and deeper into a kind of nothingness that got emptier and emptier the more it glittered. At the next interchange I took the motorway in the opposite direction, heading north. And I went even faster than I had on my escape. The further I drove, the stronger I felt. This time I was aware that nothing would stop me. The dazzling light of Langres was replaced by another that came from some place a long way ahead of me. Instead of a blinding surface that I had to protect myself from, I was being drawn by a current, luminous and sombre at the same time, tracing my route for me. It led me straight to the hospital, where I arrived just before 6 pm. As I stepped out of the car onto the asphalt of the parking lot, I had a strong sensation of unfolding, like some creature confined for a long time in too tight a skin, a chick just broken through its shell, perhaps.

With an air of authority that I was the first to find surprising, I presented myself at the reception desk as Henri Hardel's sister-in-law and asked to see his body. The girl was deep in conversation with one of her friends, but cut it short to phone through without asking any questions. Then she told me she was sorry, but there was no one there that Sunday evening, I would have to come back the next day. So I mentioned the funeral service that his widow had asked me to make arrangements for, adding that it was absolutely essential for me to view the body. I'm sure that normally I would simply have been told again to come back on Monday, but a few minutes later a young nurse came down to show me to the morgue. She opened the door to a cold, green room, like an aquarium, and seeing the drawers in the walls I had the uncomfortable feeling of being back in the vault. The nurse pulled out a drawer and Henri appeared on his tray, covered down to the knees by a white hospital gown and wearing a labelled bracelet on his left wrist. His cheeks were even more sunken, his nose and lips accordingly more prominent. What surprised me most was that he had *shrunk*, he looked like a doll. In life he'd always seemed tall, and I thought, he doesn't weigh anything any more! I stood there for a long time staring at him, while the nurse waited out in the corridor because of the cold. The words popped out all by themselves. 'You know who I am, I've come on behalf of Sabine, I've come for her . . .' And so on, babbling endlessly, my voice rising like a prayer, winding around him, imprisoning him, beseeching him. After a few moments I took his right hand, and I wasn't even frightened by its icy touch. I gripped it, still talking. 'You have to do something for your wife, Henri. Don't be a bastard. Wherever you are, do something for her. Tell me the code for the safety-deposit box.'

I couldn't swear that his lips moved, that his body heard me. But I felt my words coming back to me through him, as if at that moment his soul, or what living spark remained in him, was making its way towards me, finding refuge in me. So I stood there quietly for a long time, then I put Henri's hand back on his chest and left. It wasn't until I rejoined the nurse that the cold hit me. My whole body was trembling, and as I shivered I had a revelation. Henri, you're a simple man, Henri, you don't like words and PIE was important to you. So you won't have made much of a change.

The next morning, at about ten, I went into the vault. I entered EIP and when I turned the key everything opened smoothly, noiselessly. The light that came on automatically when the door opened lit up an Ali Baba's cave. Diamonds, banknotes, cold coins, in an eerie yellow glow, and I said, 'Henri, Henri, you're with us.' I opened the little black bag and filled it so fast it overflowed.

Then I moved on to the big Adidas bag. It was very heavy because of the gold bars and coins. I went back upstairs trying not to screw up my face with the effort or to look at anyone, still bathed in the same light that had come to me at Langres. I put the bags on the front seat of the Golf and I got to Ohain at around midday. I ran to Sabine's straight away, but she wasn't there: she was probably arranging the funeral. I carried the two bags into my daughter's room and opened them. I spread out the bundles of banknotes and the diamonds on the bed, put the gold bars, the coins and the jewels on the floor, and laid out on a low table the papers, a green notebook and the key to another safety-deposit box (number 37, at the same bank). I did a rough count of the money: there were several million francs. But I had no idea what the rings, the sapphires or the emeralds might be worth. I did recognise a blue-gold Patek Philippe among the watches, though; I liked it so much that it was hard not to put it on. But I didn't take anything, not even the smallest banknote. Less out of honesty than because I wanted to keep the full impact of my triumph.

I found plenty to do until the evening, especially in the garden, where I sprayed the roses for aphids. At about six a car pulled up, and Sabine got out with two other people, a man and a woman, younger than her. Henri's niece? They drove off again after a few minutes, and that's when I went to knock on her door.

Sabine had been to the funeral and was exhausted, her face sallow and her eyes red. She didn't seem surprised to see me.

'It's all over,' she murmured, without inviting me to sit down.

'I opened the safety-deposit box,' I answered quietly.

She looked at me, nodding, as if it wasn't important.

'Come and see, then you'll understand.'

We took the champagne into my daughter Marie's room and, as the evening sun glittered on the rings, the banknotes and even in our glasses, we felt as though we'd left the planet.

'Oh, it was so sad to see him go,' Sabine said, weeping. And then, straight after, 'But I hope he never comes back. And all that money,' she added, laughing.

'What a bastard he was,' she said a few minutes later. 'But he did think of me at the end. That's what you told me, Pauline?'

'Yes, that's what I told you.'

We drank for over an hour, laughing and crying, and then Sabine went home with the key to the other safety-deposit box and the green notebook. The next morning, she came back and asked me to go and open it: she'd found something in the notebook that must be the combination.

And so I set off again for Rue Sainte-Catherine, and opened the box on my first try. I took out seven million in cash, some stamp collections, some jewellery, and documents relating to the acquisition of major holdings in a number of jewellery firms in Antwerp. There was also a piece of paper listing the contents of the first box

I'd opened, number 35. I congratulated myself on not having been a thieving magpie. In fact, when Sabine did a count, she discovered the total on the paper wasn't correct: I'd brought her more than Henri had recorded. In the second box, we found one of those cardboard beer mats from a bar. On it, around the words STELLA ARTOIS, Henri had written in blue ink: 'On my death, I bequeath all my possessions to my de facto wife, Sabine Vandermeulen, for as long as she lives. Signed at Waterloo, the 18th of April 1997.' (See, Sabine, he did think about you.) It was a hand-written will and Sabine would be able to have it validated, especially since the lawyer didn't have another one. What really upset her, though, was the 'as long as she lives'. That meant the eventual heir would be Henri's niece, and in the meantime Sabine wouldn't be able to do just as she liked with the property entrusted to her.

I intervened once more. We were drinking port at nightfall again. I was looking at the beer mat and imagining that Henri had scribbled on it in some bar, probably after he'd had a few, and then hadn't wanted to throw it away. And hadn't been brave enough to draw up a will with a lawyer either.

'This little mat,' I said to Sabine, 'is his way of being married *behind the church*.'

She shook her head, not understanding me. I went on, 'What pen did he use to write this?'

She smiled, got up and went to get something from the bedroom. She came back with an old Mont Blanc pen and a sheet of paper.

I took it and wrote a few letters on the page. It was the same fountain-pen, the same ink.

'What are you up to?' Sabine asked me.

'I'm going to cross out the words "for as long as she lives".'

And that's what I did. I made them illegible. After that, all we had to do was submit this will to the authorities for probate. It took two months, but everything turned out OK.

Sabine told the tax department about only part of the contents of the two boxes. And the lawyer dug up proof among Henri's papers that there were seven other safety-deposit boxes, some of them in Holland. They were opened by the banks, and the money Sabine got from the first two paid the death duties. Sabine Vandermeulen had become a rich woman.

I wear jewellery now and I wish my father could see it. Sabine gave it to me, including the blue-gold Patek Philippe watch I'd wanted so much. And sometimes, when I've been away and am nodding off in the taxi home, she calls me on her mobile: she's sent a caterer to my house, and all kinds of delicacies are waiting for me. There'll be glasses of golden champagne, ruby wine, caviar on tiny plates decorated with lapis lazuli, glistening wild salmon, exotic emerald fruits. If I protest, she always says the same thing: 'Without you, I'd be on the street.'

I don't know why she wants to believe this so much. I don't know why she keeps telling me that when she dies I'll inherit everything.

A MESSAGE FOR YOU

It's like when you give up smoking, you think you know what you're missing. You line up your pencils on the table, then the cup, the eraser, the Twink, the sheets of paper and, when you've made a good start on your work, your hand reaches out for something that's not there. You think to yourself: it's looking for the packet of fags. Yes, that's what you think to yourself, because you've forgotten that the fags were already a cover-up for missing something else, so you wouldn't let it get to you. It's not exactly a smokescreen, either.

'Wait,' says Charlotte on the phone. 'There's some crazy old lady across from me, on the other side of the street. D'you know what she's done, in this heat? She's put a mattress up to block her whole window. It must be so dark inside, it must really stink. I can see her there, pulling back the net curtains in the corner, in the little space between the mattress and the wall. I'd better step back from my window. Can you hear me less clearly now? I expected that, it's clearest next to the window, but I don't want her to catch me spying on her.'

Charlotte explains that this old lady, who's always in her dressing-gown, who's shut inside her flat in the middle of August with the temperature over thirty degrees, this old lady reaches outside from time to time, just her hand, to water the geraniums on her balcony; but if she sees Charlotte, she pulls back in a hurry, 'as if she was frightened of me'.

Charlotte shakes her head, a bit discouraged. This neighbourhood is getting impossible. She mentions the tramp, sitting on the park bench between the pigeon droppings, near Boulevard Pasteur. She plucked up her courage and spoke to him, yesterday, and it was as if he were emerging from the ocean mists to answer her, talking gibberish, a mixture of three languages, Lithuanian, English and French. He used to live on board ships – as good a way as any of living nowhere. Hardly surprising that he's got nothing left to share with anyone, except his stench, of course. Actually, everyone's stewing in their own juice.

At the other end of the line, her colleague is already answering in monosyllables. Old people on their own in August and tramps, she's not all that interested.

But, almost as soon as she's finished the phone call, Charlotte is aware that her hand is searching for something again. It's not reaching out for a cigarette, even if in fact she'd quite like one. What she's missing is her daughter, and her daughter knows this window well. Because this was Julie's exit for climbing down and joining her boyfriend at all hours of the night, right through the winter. Easy, there was some plasterer's scaffolding. After the scaffolding was taken down and Charlotte found out what she was up to (in any case her schoolwork was such a mess that her escapades couldn't have gone on unnoticed for long, especially with the dark circles under her eyes getting bigger by the day), Julie threatened to jump straight out of the window. Then, when she didn't have the nerve for that, she swallowed her mother's sleeping tablets.

Her father was wild with rage. Mad at Charlotte, of course: 'Haven't you learned yet that you can't just leave sleeping pills lying around?' They're on holiday together, Julie, her father and her father's new family. Several times tonight Charlotte's hand has tapped out the number for their house on Oléron Island. And, when Julie finally answered, she just said, 'Everything's fine, Mum, we're going to have a barbecue, the weather's fantastic, big hug, talk to you later.'

Afterwards, emptiness again. She goes out, goes to see a Robert Altman film again, one she'd really liked but now all she remembers is its vaguely oppressive atmosphere and the title, *Shortcuts*. What really matters, she thinks, is that the cinema has air-conditioning.

The next morning, when she opened the sitting-room window before heading off to the lab, she noticed a string hanging down from the old lady's balcony. On the end of the string was a piece of paper. It's a very narrow street and at this hour there was no sunlight and no breeze. And yet the paper was spinning slowly: when it bumped against the stone wall beneath the first-floor window it swung out again as if wounded by the contact. Impossible to read what was written on it. This crumpled piece of paper, covered in dust, could only mean bad news. A call for help. The old lady probably didn't have a long enough piece of string – whatever the reason, the message was too high up for people walking along the footpath. And as for the first-floor tenants, who could have just reached out and grabbed the string, they were away on holiday. It followed then – Charlotte couldn't help reasoning this out, which irritated her, as if she was already being forced into something – that the message was at her height and that it must be meant for her. For her, Charlotte Simon, who had no desire to be mixed up in this business. She went off to work, hoping that her irritation would help her forget all about the piece of paper or, better yet, that someone else would have the bright idea of taking it down.

It was very pleasant at the lab. Most of Charlotte's colleagues were on holiday, she felt that she had immense amounts of time at her disposal, and even, rather deliciously, that she was some kind of illegal immigrant. And it's when you're an illegal that you cross boundaries, allow yourself to make discoveries.

The closest researcher to her office was none other than Fabrice Baugé, aka Back from the Dead. As she passed, Charlotte saw him, pepper-and-salt beard, sitting in front of his computer. Baugé had had an astonishing career, becoming famous very early for a project he'd carried out at the start of the eighties, a study of paternity in three countries, the US, the UK and France. Baugé had been in charge of the French segment. The American results had come in first: based on analysis of the DNA of newborn babies (using the RFLP technique applied to Jeffreys's probes), thirty-three per cent of the infants studied were not the children of their presumed fathers. Using the same protocol in maternity hospitals in the Lyon area, Baugé had obtained an even more stupefying result – thirty-seven per cent were not the children of their presumed fathers, and one and a half per cent weren't even the offspring of their supposed mothers! This latter figure was thought to be the result of accidental switching of babies in the maternity hospitals. These findings were so devastating for the generally accepted concept of the family that the scientific community subjected them to lengthy scrutiny and criticism, but didn't manage to refute them. Much later Charlotte learned from a biologist friend that the blood samples used by Baugé came from old stocks taken at the start of the seventies, and that the donors' social circumstances were not really known. But Baugé's reputation, once established, stayed with him. And even if his findings had never shaken Charlotte's beliefs, she thought there was something heroic, something naively grandiose in this act of submitting paternity to scientific testing. As if someone had had the nerve to try to prove through abstract scientific reasoning and with the aid of machines and test tubes that Julie's father was indeed the man Charlotte and everyone else believed he was.

That wasn't all: due to another extraordinary set of circumstances, Baugé had been struck down at the age of fifty-two by Parkinson's disease, not only rapidly progressing but also massively incapacitating. He had the shakes, could barely speak, couldn't walk any more and was confined to his home, where his wife became his nurse. And then, last April, he'd been miraculously cured by one of the first attempts in France at neuro-surgical treatment of the disease. The success of the operation had surpassed all expectations, and since the summer Fabrice Baugé could walk and talk and didn't have the shakes any more. He'd come back to his work in the lab. A tall, bony man, he'd let his beard grow while he was sick, and had decided not to shave it off when he recovered; it made him look like some lost prophet. Even his clothes dated from his pre-Parkinson's days. His resurrection gave him an aura that sometimes made his colleagues feel uneasy. He moved slowly and spoke little. When Charlotte greeted him he told her, in such a slow, deep voice that it sounded as if it were prerecorded: 'We're all on our own.'

At midday Charlotte ate by herself at the Grillon. She liked its old-fashioned frontage, the double wooden doors with their glass panels and the name of the restaurant in green and black lettering on the lintel, and most of all its old-fashioned, almost country-style atmosphere with the two fans, one on the counter and the other at the back of the room next to a ficus tree, the long tables and the waitress with her tanned arms, still dreaming of sun, sea and sand. Although she was close to home, Charlotte drove back to the lab without even going down her street.

When she got home at around 5 pm, the letter was still hanging there, about four metres up. If she had a long stick she could easily get it down, but she didn't want to go out and get a stick and then find herself on her own in the street trying to deal with this emergency before it was too late. She looked around. The few passers-by on Rue Falguière hurried past without seeing anything, each in their own little world. She swore under her breath, everyone's so indifferent, here in Paris, that you could slit the throats of an entire family without being disturbed. She walked back up to the bakery that had just been repainted; now a scroll on the window, decorated with musical notes, announced the superior qualities of traditional-style bread. Charlotte preferred another bakery, on Rue Dulac, but that one was closed for the summer holidays.

Once inside the shop, if she leaned a little she could still make out the string and the piece of white paper. She waited her turn behind a mother buying lollipops for her two children. The baker's wife, sweating and as red as if she were in a rage, sported a mechanical, one-sided smile. On the glass panel in front of the croissants and the bread rolls was sellotaped an enlarged copy of a newspaper article: BAKER KNEADED PLASTIQUE TOO. It was about a bomb. An out-of-sorts rival had blown this bakery up. Charlotte hadn't known a thing about it. She'd thought it was just a fire.

'Oh my,' she said. 'Strange goings-on in the neighbourhood.'

The baker's wife turned her half-grin on Charlotte.

'D'you see that string over there?' Charlotte asked, clearing her throat.

The other woman looked surprised, then turned with a frown in the direction Charlotte was pointing. 'What is it?' she asked, her voice completely flat. Charlotte was so put out by this indifference that she sighed, mumbled that that was exactly the problem, and left.

Back home again, she poured herself a tall glass of Pepsi (too much sugar, she knows that), and tried to get back to tidying the sitting room. For the last three days she'd been imagining a new order, one where the past wouldn't intrude constantly and unpredictably. But the first thing she picked up was a pencil case made of varnished wood, the one old Madame Desmeures had given Julie back in the days when they lived in Rue César Franck. The very same Madame Desmeures who'd starved to death over the month of August when everyone was away on holiday. And the concierge of the building, back from Spain, couldn't stop saying how shocking it was: 'She had loads of beautiful things in her flat. She could easily have sold them. And her furniture! It all got sold off afterwards, anyway. She couldn't take it with her . . .'

Yes, why don't people sell off their memories with all the rest of their stuff?

She opened the pencil case. The name Elisabeth Desmeures was painted in gold letters inside the lid. On a bed of blue velvet lay a shiny, round-bellied pen-holder, its nib dull and ink-stained.

Even this keepsake led Charlotte back to the old lady across the street. Like some kind of conspiracy. Unable to help herself, she went back downstairs, looked this way and that, then walked towards the photographer's at the end of the street. If the window display was anything to go by, the owner took an interest in what was going on around him. He'd put on display a series of black-and-white photos of the neighbourhood businesses. The first thing you noticed, among the pictures of shops, workshops and tradespeople (and in black-and-white they had an archetypal, nostalgic look about them, something beyond the realm of colour), was Lemaître's wine bar, the owner in a grey or blue apron, his hand resting on a cask, looking proud and distant with his droopy moustache. The next photo was of Gilles Guglielmi, hairdresser. Guglielmi had white hair in a crewcut and looked a bit like a former boxer because of his broken nose. But he'd been smart enough to take on two ravishing female assistants. The plain caption read: *Hair Salon of Monsieur Guglielmi, Award-Winning Stylist*. Then Madame El Charid and her husband in the tiny workshop where they did alterations, standing between the jackets on their hangers, behind a very old sewing-machine, a Singer, with a black metal wheel like a steering wheel, which did duty as a shop sign. A little lower down, a couple whose caption announced that they'd been running the laundry on Boulevard Pasteur for more than thirty years. They were both smiling sweetly, he standing behind the counter with his arms crossed, she with her bosom overhanging the scales used to weigh the washing. But what really stood out was the photographer himself, Gérard Bosquet. He was holding a print in his hand: a copy of the one in the window. Charlotte smiled at this reference to the tradition of the self-portrait within the self-portrait. At the same time she wondered how it was possible to photograph a photo which doesn't yet exist. Looking at Gérard Bosquet's sly expression, she understood that he must be enjoying this paradox. She went into the shop and, as soon as the photographer came towards her (easily recognisable now that she'd studied the window display), she told him she lived three doors away. 'Over there,' she said, her arm outstretched. When he looked in the direction of her pointing finger, she added, 'Over there, do you see that string and that piece of paper? Well, that's across from where I live.' She tried to explain the situation to him, and asked him to come and help her retrieve the message. Bosquet was tall, a step-stool would do the trick. But Bosquet scratched his moustache, looked around, he was on his own. 'I can't leave the shop,' he grumbled.

'Not even for just a few moments? Not even if you put a notice up saying, Back in two minutes, like the hairdresser on Rue Nicolas-Charlet does all the time? If any customers come you'll see them quite easily from over there.'

He took a deep breath, tipped his head back and pinched his nose as if sniffing out some trick. 'No,' he said, at length. 'Let's wait and see if the paper's still there at closing time. I'll have my apprentice here then, she's the one who does the passport photos.' And he gave Charlotte a piercing look, to show her he wasn't going to let her put one over on him.

She left the shop, feeling a little ashamed at having attracted such suspicion. She stood for a moment at the end of the street, thinking about whether to go and get her own steps. No, no, no! She stopped in front of the plumber's; his workshop hadn't been featured in Bosquet's portrait gallery. With good reason, too, probably: it wasn't much to look at – a tiny office half-hidden by a big green awning. The sign on the door, in black plastic stick-on lettering, read MEYRINCK PLUMBING 01 43 21 88 43. He was the plumber for Charlotte's building and he'd been to her flat before. She went in. Meyrinck, a curly-haired fat man, was sitting at his workbench, looking for something in a jumble of invoices, rubber joints, suppliers' pamphlets and clamp collars, and talking to his workman. They turned towards her at the same time. 'Here's the problem,' Charlotte said, starting to explain it all over again. It was taking more and more energy to tell people what was bothering her, and she was overwhelmed by a feeling that she was talking into thin air. The two plumbers went over to the window. Heads together as if they were plotting something, they watched the paper swaying on the end of the string.

'Hadn't you noticed it?' she asked, an anguished lump making her throat feel tight.

'It's too high up,' Meyrinck announced, not answering her question.

'No, I'll do it, I've got my ladder on the van,' the workman said. He went out straight away, pulled the ladder from the roof of the little white van parked just outside, propped it against the wall of the building and was back half a minute later with the piece of paper he'd pulled off. 'Here you go,' he said to Charlotte, very pleased with himself.

'You see how easy that was,' she told Meyrinck sadly. She stood there, feeling a bit stupid, then thanked them and went up to her flat.

On the piece of paper, a crookedly cut half-page, were written some names and addresses, like this:

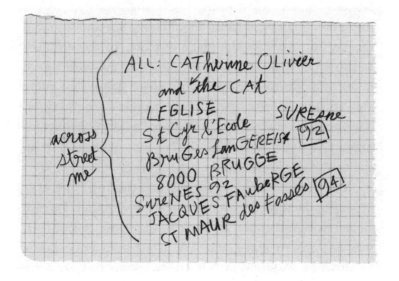

Charlotte spent quite some time studying this message. The writing didn't seem incoherent, except that there were upper and lower case letters within the same word and the writing seemed to slant to the left, which really focused attention on the words 'across street me'. She's across on the left, and on the right the others are lined up. All the others, the Léglises, Catherine, Olivier, the Jacques Fauberge family, and the cat. The cat as well. Even the cat, she thought sadly. Especially the cat. (And me too, across from her.)

In the directory, Charlotte found an Olivier Léglise in Suresnes. She called the number and got an answering machine. She didn't like to leave a message and told herself she'd call again later. There was also a Jacques Fauberge living in Saint-Maur. This time the phone rang and rang, no answer. Away on holiday, maybe. Jacques Fauberge, left in the lurch, she grumbled as she hung up. The easiest thing would have been to signal to the hermit, to wave the piece of paper in the window to show her that she had it and she was trying to figure it out. Charlotte went out onto the balcony but there was no sign of life across the street on the second floor. The mattress was squarely in place, its greyish buttons pressing against the glass as the last rays of the sun lit up the top of the building like a fiery lake.

She went back to her sorting and tidying. The next morning she took the message to work with her. Fabrice Baugé was still there, in exactly the same position. It was enough to make you wonder if he'd gone home at all since yesterday. Charlotte went to talk to him, enormously, absurdly hopeful, as if a man who had almost left this world ought to be able to see things more clearly than mere mortals. He listened to her, his eyes half-closed (it was hot, the air-conditioning was still on the blink), nodding away (Charlotte wouldn't have been surprised if he'd started to drool), then suddenly he perked up, grabbed the piece of paper, laid it flat and smoothed it out so hard that Charlotte was afraid he was going to tear it.

'I get her meaning,' he grunted. Then, 'You've probably looked up the Léglises in Suresnes and the Fauberges in Saint-Maur in the book?'

'Yes, of course.'

'Well, they're not home. No one's home, except you.'

She was speechless for a moment. 'Are you kidding me?'

He shook his head. 'No,' he said, 'that's exactly what the message means.'

She felt her knees go weak, as if the Delphic oracle had just spoken. It was a good thing Baugé was staring at the ceiling.

She swallowed. 'At least look at the layout,' she begged. 'What can you say about that? That bracket thing on the left, don't you think that symbolises that she's shut in?'

'What's the point of symbolising it,' he rumbled, 'when she is shut in, it's a fact.'

Charlotte's lips muttered 'Thanks', but in her heart she was cursing Baugé.

When she got home, she saw a new piece of paper dangling from the second-floor balcony. Thirty centimetres higher than yesterday's, and yet it was the same piece of string. And again Charlotte couldn't make anything out at this distance.

I'm not touching this one, she promised herself.

Half an hour later, she was picturing the old lady in her death throes, struggling to breathe in the stale air of her room. It was unbearable.

That old cow is going to ruin my whole week! She phoned her mother. Just to see how she was, but she couldn't help telling her about her elderly neighbour. 'She's all on her own in the dark, and throwing out messages into the sea.'

Her mother wasn't a woman to be easily deterred. She was down to one lung, but she kept on smoking. She was American. When she was quite young she'd worked in military intelligence. Sent off to England during the war, she'd fallen madly in love with an English pilot who was killed on a mission three months after they were married. In a sense, her life had ended there. She'd married a Frenchman (Charlotte's father) in 1950, but she had no qualms about saying he was a consolation prize that hadn't consoled her much. Charlotte was the child of her mother's resignation; she'd talked about this a lot with her analyst, and now all that remained was a kind of dull pain and a pride in being able to live even though she was the product of something 'second best'.

'Call the emergency services,' her mother told her,

sounding full of energy. 'They'll come and get it sorted. If they have to they'll smash in the door and tear down the message. Or else . . .'

There was a silence.

'Or else I'll come over tomorrow and we'll sort it out.'

'Thank you,' Charlotte said. She didn't have enough strength left for irony.

She called the emergency services. They refused to send a squad for a little piece of string. As for the old lady, there was no clear indication that she needed assistance. 'Call again if anything changes.'

The police, then. The administrator on the end of the line was unhelpful, unpleasant. Carefully took down Charlotte's details, then, 'We can't take action unless there's a disturbance of the peace.'

'But there is a disturbance,' she shouted. 'Someone's in distress, don't you find that disturbing? More than noise? Wouldn't you take action if there was excessive noise?'

Silence.

'It's keeping me awake at night.'

'I'm very sorry, Madame. You could call in and fill out a complaint, if you like.'

She went downstairs to the plumber's. She pointed to the new message. 'Another message for you, is it?' he said, irritably. 'I don't believe it, it's just like Hotmail!' He changed tack and, serious, said, 'I haven't got a ladder, my workman's not here.' Then he went back to making phone calls as if Charlotte wasn't there either.

★

The next day the message was still dangling at the end of the string, looking a little the worse for wear. Charlotte's mother arrived just before ten. Khaki trousers, white shirt, sneakers and a green beret. 'You look like an agent from *Special Mission*,' Charlotte told her. Her mother smiled and lit up a Camel Light. She seemed to be in great shape, apart from one shoulder, on the same side as her lung operation, hunching forward a bit.

'Let's go,' commanded the woman of action, speaking in English. Charlotte had always pretended that she didn't understand this language very well. Despite three extended stays in the States, she spoke with such a dreadfully French accent that her mother had offered to pay for psychotherapy sessions for her.

They strode across the street. Standing beneath the piece of paper, the mother (whose name was Ruth) made a guess at how high it was. 'Too high for the step-stool,' she decided. Then, hands on hips, she studied the door of the building intently. Even the wrinkles on her neck seemed to strain to the task.

'In the old days,' she said, 'I knew a guy who could climb straight up the wall of a house and get in through any window.'

'Spiderman.'

'That wasn't his code-name,' said Ruth, trying to remember.

Two crazy ladies. Charlotte couldn't stand being in her mother's company for long. She felt the urge to run away. One day she'd turn into one of those lonely old women who feed the pigeons. But she really hated pigeons.

No one came out of the building, no one went in. Ruth stepped back onto the roadway. 'Why didn't the woman tie on another piece of string?' she asked suddenly. 'You'd think she doesn't want anyone to get their hands on her message. Yoo hoo, up there!' she shouted, waving her arms.

No sign of life behind the mattress.

'Come with me to the pharmacy,' Ruth said. 'I'm sure the chemist's assistant will know something.'

Ruth knew this pharmacy well: it was where she bought the Phoscol® tonic that kept her so mentally alert in spite of the cancer and being seventy-eight.

'I'd rather wait for you at home,' Charlotte said.

'Ah ha!' Ruth responded sharply. 'You don't want to know how to gather intelligence? You don't know what you're missing.'

Half an hour later, Ruth came back up the stairs. She was a bit out of breath but pretty pleased with herself.

'Her name's Marcotte,' she said, 'but I didn't get her first name. She picks up tranquillisers at the chemist's on a regular basis. She has a prescription from the psychiatric services on Rue de Vaugirard. The problem is, the centre is closed for the whole of August and she's all on her own. No one's seen her for three weeks.'

'That's exactly what I told you,' Charlotte answered. 'Then at least we know there'll be someone to look out for her in a while . . . If she doesn't die before then.'

'Yes, well, we can find out more about her.'

'How?'

'From the hairdresser at the top of Boulevard Pasteur. If you like, we can go and see him.'

'The hairdresser?' Charlotte hesitated. Now that her mother was there, the situation seemed less urgent. She was starting to think it was bad manners to stick her nose into the old lady's life like this. 'What could this hairdresser do?'

'He knows her pretty well. Apparently he's related to her somehow.'

'In that case, she doesn't need us.'

Her mother sat down, took out another cigarette.

'Couldn't you stop smoking, in front of me at least?' Charlotte said.

Ruth carried on as if she hadn't heard her. Her short, silvery hair had a touch of blue tint to stop it from looking yellow.

'This hairdresser strikes me as a bit of an oddball. He used to live in Algeria, apparently.'

Charlotte didn't answer. She thought about the picture of Gilles Guglielmi in the photographer's window display.

'Let's go and see him,' said her mother.

'No,' Charlotte replied. 'I just wanted to get the piece of paper down, that's all.'

Her nose was out of joint. The message was addressed to her, and in less than an hour her mother had barged in and taken over.

'Shame,' said her mother. 'You'll never know the

truth. We're about to crack it, and you want to just flag it away?'

Charlotte wouldn't meet her eyes.

'You know,' Ruth continued, 'patients have died from this, out in the country, from a couple of surgeons not communicating properly. You should always put other people's welfare before your own.'

'I know, I know. That's how you won the war.'

'That's also how France lost it,' Ruth hit back. She had so much self-assurance! Charlotte hated that Anglo-Saxon way of always giving the moral high ground to the winner.

'What's Dad up to?' she asked suddenly.

'Watercolours, this morning.'

'Won't he be bored without you?'

Ruth sighed and shook her head. 'You want me to leave, is that it?' She stood up, stiffly. The energy she'd had earlier had melted away. She was getting old and weak again. She coughed.

'I'm sorry,' Charlotte said.

'You've never let me help you,' her mother said.

'I'm really sorry I took it badly. All right then, let's go and see this hairdresser.'

They didn't speak at all during the short walk. Alone in his salon, Guglielmi was sitting in one of the chairs with his feet up on a green leather footstool, reading the *Figaro* newspaper. The two women stopped for a moment in front of the shop window: below the big white letters of GILLES, LADIES' AND GENTS' HAIRDRESSER was displayed a photo of the man himself, shaking hands with Jean Tibéri, Mayor of Paris, who was awarding him a medal for services to French hairdressing. Despite his age, he leaped to his feet to greet the two women. But with a wave of the hand Ruth indicated that she hadn't come for a haircut, and in her best American French informed him that the chemist had sent her and her daughter.

'Because of Madame Marcotte,' she added.

'Mar-cotte,' Charlotte said, enunciating carefully.

'You mean the . . .'

'The lady who lives over there, in the street down the hill,' Ruth said, 'at number 12.'

'Oh yes?'

'She's got a problem,' said Ruth.

'Oh yes? Rachel Marcotte, I know her. So what about her?'

'Well, she's sending signals to my daughter. Messages on a piece of string.'

Charlotte showed him the piece of paper.

The hairdresser sighed, scratched his head, adjusted his glasses, studied the paper.

'Oh yes,' he said. 'This one, Catherine Léglise, that's her sister, eh. And this one, here, Jacques Fauberge, he's the husband of her other sister, the one who, um, passed away, ah, beside her bed.'

Charlotte and Ruth looked at each other. He had a strange way of putting things.

'So she's not short of family,' Ruth said.

'She's afraid of them, of her family,' the hairdresser said. 'She's defending herself, shielding herself. They shoot laser beams at her, don't they, so she puts up the mattress.'

'Laser beams?' asked Charlotte.

'She's cut them out of her will. From what she says, they want to take over her apartment and throw her into the street.'

Silence.

'And what about you, is she frightened of you?' Ruth asked.

'I'm a cousin, that's all. A distant cousin.'

'Uh huh,' said Ruth, frowning.

Through his thick lenses, he looked her straight in the eye, his mouth twisted in a little smile.

'I can give you the door code for the building. If you don't believe me, go on up and see her, she'll put you in the picture. There's something, how shall I put it, suggestive, about her. Very, very suggestive. But she won't let go. That's the problem, eh.'

'She won't let go?' asked Charlotte, feeling more and more confused.

'I swear to you, like a dog with a whatsit, bone,' Guglielmi said, running his hand through his white hair. 'If I go to see her – yes, sure, I do go sometimes – she's like a dog, growls, bares her teeth. Like this.'

He grimaced, baring his gums. The women stepped back. He invited them to sit down and have a cup of coffee, an offer they turned down in unison.

'She won't let it go,' he went on. 'She's doing it to frighten me. I've known her since childhood, see, she was in Algeria with me when I was a kid. Let me tell you something, I was behind at school because of a dog. It bit me, eh. It tore out one of my eyes when I was two and a half, and after that, hey, dogs just scared the hell out of me. That figures, right?'

'Yes, of course. So she plays on your fear. But you've still got your eye,' Ruth remarked.

'They put it back in. But it was still Rachel, my cousin, who looked after me. I was too scared, I couldn't learn any more. That's what people did to me, eh. When they saw me with one eye hanging down my cheek, they said, that's the end of him. And you know, that can kill you. Like that cyclist here, on the footpath the other day. He fell down head-first into a coma, and the passers-by were saying, "He's dead." And you know, that could kill him. It's really serious. So you can't say something silly to her either. It could kill her.'

'But we haven't said a thing about her,' Charlotte protested.

'She's lost her focus. Except with me, she shows me her teeth. Because of other people's, whatsit, acrimosity. You see, in life, you need quiet strength. I know what I'm talking about, because I used to be a boxer. Look,' he said, brandishing a pair of scissors. 'I can cut hair with my eyes shut, if I focus properly. I can even split hairs if you want. But if I'm not, whatsit, focused, I'm blind even if my eyes are open, and I'll cut your skin. It's the same with boxing, eh. I throw ten punches and I just tickle you. And then I really focus and bam! I can flatten a bull. In those days they didn't know enough about psychology to understand that.'

The two women nodded. The hairdresser was gazing out past them now, out beyond the boulevard even.

'Rachel's frightened of being robbed, how do you say it, possessed, no, dispossessed. We're living in a century of thieves. Let me give you an example. I was watching TV the other night, and I says to my wife, there you go, they've pinched my script idea again. It's all about making a profit, these days, and no one's any the wiser.'

He started telling them some story about a man from another planet who was living in a bombed-out church and who eventually saved humanity, ravaged by wars and money. In the end this saviour turned out to be Jewish.

'That was your script?' Ruth asked.

'Did they show that on TV?' Charlotte wondered.

'You betcha. But I shouldn't tell my ideas to my customers. Afterwards it gets to Hollywood, and the upshot is that I get to pay to see what someone's stolen from me. I'm not saying this to get at you,' he added suddenly, putting his hand on his heart and looking at Ruth. 'I've got nothing against Americans. The opposite, in fact.'

'Fine, fine,' said Ruth. 'Can you give us your cousin's door code? So we can go up and see her.'

He looked it up in a notebook full of pages with their corners turned down, and that's when Charlotte noticed that the salon was in a pretty poor state. There was hair still lying unswept on the floor, some of the towels had holes in them, the chairs were worn. Scissors, combs and razors were soaking in jars of blueish antiseptic, like little bodies floating in formalin, sending out glowing yellow signals from time to time as the sun shone in through the window.

'Actually,' Charlotte said, 'there's another message from your cousin still hanging in front of her building. Would you mind helping me to get it down?'

He looked at her, his pale blue eyes made huge by the lenses of his glasses. 'Oh no, that's bad luck. You should never touch the misfortune of the hanged.'

Charlotte pulled a face. Ruth stood up, held out her hand to the hairdresser and said, with great dignity, 'May I thank you, sir, for your courageous assistance in ensuring the wellness, the – how do you say it, Charlotte?'

'Welfare.'

'In ensuring the welfare of your cousin.'

'No problem,' Gilles Guglielmi declared. Smiling modestly, he shook her hand, just the way he'd smiled and shaken hands with Jean Tibéri.

They went back out into the street. 'And now,' Ruth announced, 'you have to go to the city council and inform social services. The woman's crazy, they might pack her off somewhere. In any case, it won't be your problem any more.'

'No, no way,' said Charlotte.

'I might've known,' her mother said. 'If I hadn't said anything, you'd have done it on your own initiative.'

'No,' Charlotte repeated.

They said goodbye on the corner of Rue Falguière. Charlotte carried on as far as her building, then looked up towards her windows. To go on up the street, see the mattress again, the string, the bony hand waving to her . . . It was unbearable. She wavered for a moment longer on the footpath, then crossed over to number 12, where she tapped in the door code the hairdresser had given her. She was almost surprised to see the door open. She took a deep breath and went over to the lift. It was out of order. No wonder the old lady stays upstairs, she said to herself, clinging to this reasonable explanation.

She knew which door it was straight away, even though there was no nameplate on it. Something about its position, and the obvious thickness of the wood, the huge lock and the metal corner plates; a prison door. The first time she rang, there was no sign of life. Only to be expected. Charlotte was even prepared to go away empty-handed, leaving a note to say she would try again tomorrow. And tomorrow she would see if her note was still sitting there.

She stood her ground directly in front of the peephole so that Rachel Marcotte would have plenty of time to inspect her and perhaps recognise her. She rang again. Thirty seconds later she shouted into the tiny gap between the door and the jamb: 'I'm your neighbour, I've got a message for you.' No response. As she moved towards the stairs she heard a key turn in the lock. She turned around. There was a click as the door opened part-way. Since it was even darker in the apartment than on the landing, it was hard to make out the person standing in the opening.

'Madame Marcotte?' Charlotte called softly.

The door opened wider and the shape became clearer.

'I'm your neighbour from across the street,' said Charlotte, taking two steps forward.

The woman in the tartan dressing-gown was quite solidly built, her grey hair wild. She stared at Charlotte, her little eyes dark and sharp.

'You sent me a message,' Charlotte said. 'May I speak to you?'

'To me?' The voice was rasping, agitated. They stood there face to face for a few seconds, then Madame Marcotte stepped back and gestured to Charlotte to come in, with that same skinny arm she used to stick out of the window. Charlotte moved past her and let the door swing shut. Her throat felt tight. At the end of the hallway, Madame Marcotte opened the door into the sitting room. It was lit by a lamp sitting on a low table and by the light coming through the gap – a vertical band about ten centimetres wide – between the mattress and the window frame. A glass-fronted dresser, its usual place outlined against the left-hand wall, was now propping up the mattress. In front of the dresser, a kitchen table with two chairs. On the table, an empty bottle of mineral water, a TV remote control and a boning knife. The effect of the dresser in front of the window was to refocus the room around the opposite corner, dominated by the lamp with its round green pottery base and a glowing orange shade. Around the lamp were displayed photographs in rounded frames. The overall impression was of a sanctuary. Madame Marcotte pointed Charlotte towards the two-seater sofa against the right-hand wall and sat down, or rather let herself fall onto one of the chairs. Her expression had changed: she looked tired and anxious. She kept rubbing her left thumb and index finger together.

'It's cool in here,' Charlotte said, 'but it's dark.'

'You see,' said Rachel Marcotte, 'you see.'

'It feels a bit . . . other-worldly, here.'

Madame Marcotte stared at her and said, 'You can't live in a tomb just because people want to kill you.'

But that's what you're doing, Charlotte wanted to reply. She was feeling weary too.

'It's life that wants to kill us,' she said.

'Life, life, life's nothing. I'm fighting,' Madame Marcotte said, 'instead of dying. They want to kill me, and if I kill myself, if I kill myself with that, for example,' she added, pointing to the knife on the table, 'or if I jump out of the window, they'll have won. So I resist.'

'Why do they want to kill you?'

'Do they even know the reason themselves? D'you think people get killed for a real reason? They find a reason, but before that they hate them. Children get killed because they're not the way they wanted them to be. But they don't know how they wanted them to be.'

Charlotte felt incapable of interpreting so much

good sense. Rachel Marcotte's grating voice seemed like an unanswerable complaint. But she wasn't any threat.

'You see,' the same rasping voice went on (and yet there were no cigarettes, no smell of cigarette smoke), 'I'm very normal: I live so as not to die. But I'm not normal because I'm aware of it. That's what my family can't tolerate.'

'The mattress,' Charlotte asked, 'what does it protect you from?'

'Oh, the mattress, it's like socks. And they can poison the water, too, so I drink bottled water. And now I've run out.'

'You could order some by telephone.'

At the same time Charlotte was thinking that if the water was poisoned Madame Marcotte must be frightened to wash herself. But she didn't smell and she didn't look dirty. There were no stains on her dressing-gown.

'The telephone,' Rachel Marcotte spoke this word in a voice heavy with meaning. A silence, then she added, 'No more telephone, that way I don't have to listen to their filth.'

'All the same, it's a more convenient way to ask for help than a bit of paper on a string,' Charlotte said with a smile.

They sat for some time without speaking. Charlotte had the impression that Madame Marcotte was falling asleep. She would close her eyes, her shoulders would sag, then she would wake up again.

'That message you hung out of the window, what was that?'

Madame Marcotte jumped. 'What?'

Charlotte repeated her question.

'You didn't read it, then?' said Madame Marcotte, with a suspicious look.

'No.'

She got up, restless again, went to the window, walking sideways so she could keep her eyes fixed on Charlotte, put her hand outside and pulled up the string. 'Here,' she said, detaching the piece of paper.

Charlotte took it and read it, 'I came,' she said, stunned.

'Yes.'

'That's incredible,' Charlotte said.

Rachel Marcotte had sat down again. She was having trouble staying upright on her chair.

'You're exhausted,' said Charlotte. 'Why don't you go to bed?'

'I wish I could, but I'd need another mattress, because now they can get to me through the kitchen window.'

'Is that mattress in front of the window the one off your bed?'

Rachel nodded. 'I sleep there,' she said, pointing first at the rug beneath the table that the lamp was standing on, then at the photos. Charlotte didn't ask if the photos watched over her. Or if she turned the light out to go to sleep. She didn't want to commit herself more deeply, to go back with Rachel through memories that would certainly make her heart ache. Not today, maybe never. She got up.

'I'll go and get you some help.'

Rachel shook her head.

'You came,' she said, 'but you can't make me drink. You'll protest: "No, of course not, I won't kill you." Sadly, I know all about people like you, they kill you all the same, without realising.'

'How do you mean?'

'You'll tell them to take away my mattress.'

'Absolutely not,' Charlotte protested. 'I'm perfectly aware that it's protecting you.'

'Do you think it's stopping the laser beams from reaching me?'

'Yes, in one sense it does.'

'You're lying!' Rachel's eyes were bright with anger. 'You don't understand the first thing about it,' she continued. 'You're talking nonsense. That mattress protects me from me. It stops me from jumping. Don't you see that as long as they're against me I'm not going to kill myself?'

Charlotte nodded, giving up. So then, she thought to herself, I have to be against her too? She got up and left. Slowly.

Out in the street, she felt blinded by the light. She looked in the direction of the photographer's shop. Further on, the baker's wife, the hairdresser, the chemist, the plumber, like illustrations in a school textbook. They were screens. All of them. She was too. That much she could see, but she couldn't make out what was moving behind them.

MY BOXING CAREER

I'm reaching for him with my fists, the fight's over, I'm just trying to be friendly, but it feels as if my glove's going right through him, as if he doesn't have a body any more. Our helmets are touching and I can feel our exhaustion in the heaviness of the sweat dripping off us. Then when I straighten up I see the glazed look on David's face, as if he's afraid of getting told off. I'm glad I won, but I still think it's a shame because he's the one who's keen on boxing and it was his idea for me to come and train with him instead of mouldering away in my little room. He even managed to wangle me a discount because I'm a foreign student. But now I think we're both losers, and I want to tell him it's just luck that I won. I even want to spit out the mouth-guard and explain that he was good, better than me in the first round, he just about had me. The words were coming out of my eyes, my nose, I kept thinking, 'I'll wind up with a poem,' because it's the hard knocks that make great poets, apparently.

It all changed in the second round: every jab he threw came back at him like hitting a mirror, and I was really feeling good about coming back at him so hard; it was as if the only result of all his efforts was that my hide got thicker, I was getting lighter and lighter and stronger as well, and my fists were punching effortlessly. I was dancing. The problem, the real problem for David, is that he hasn't got the physique for boxing – maybe it's a question of balance, or muscle density. I'm sure that the body is just one form of existence, that it's no more substantial than anything else, the imagination or the soul, and that's what I'd tell him if I could.

The trainer just says, 'That's fine, you guys, you can head off now.' He's in a hurry to see the back of us, there are other, more serious customers waiting, two Kiwi blokes who belong to the club and even have big ambitions. And then when I walk in front of him he gives me a bit of a smile and asks, 'So where are you from, then?' I use the mouth-guard as an excuse for not answering. His name is Ramon, he's from the Philippines, with silvery hair around his temples. Apparently he was a pro in the States, welter-weight I think. I resent that he never remembers my name.

David goes straight to the showers but I hang around in the gym to watch the other two box. I take off my gloves and then I can't get the taping off my left hand; suddenly it won't open properly, it's a bit numb – as if it's been too tightly clenched. The sweat is still burning my eyes. No towel, just a grubby rag hanging on a bit of string. Where am I going to wipe my hands and face, then? Where? All of a sudden my voice is back and I can complain.

After a bit I feel cold because they've opened the back door. I worked out that I'd need to lose three kilos to get back down to fighting weight. Three kilos, that's a couple of medium-sized chickens, a couple of chickens too many that would fly away from somewhere inside me.

The Pakeha guy is first into the ring. He hops and skips about on his own and throws punches at some imaginary opponent; everyone does that when they box, I wonder if it's ever been any other way. I say hello because I know him – Brian – and he gives me a nod in between hops. Last week, in the other room, he showed us the comics he draws: he's got a crisp, clean line, vivid colours, really violent war scenes. One of these comics has even been published, he pulled it out of his bag with some others he was going to send to his publisher. I was pretty impressed to be standing there with a real author. There were a few of us hanging around him, but I was the only one who turned nearly all the pages and looked at them one after the other. I remember that I glanced up at him from time to time, maybe I was trying to figure out if he looked anything like what he drew. He appreciated my interest, even asked me what my name was, and repeated it, mispronouncing it a bit.

His opponent walks around the room as if he's looking for something or wanting to talk to Ramon, the trainer, who's deep in discussion with one of the club directors and doesn't notice him. In the end, he jumps into the ring, and I can see he's a pretty powerful guy, with huge pecs. Maori, maybe, or Samoan, yeah, he's built like those indestructible rugby players that can't be tackled to the ground even by two or three opponents. He's got rounded muscles that glisten under the lights, a tattoo glowing on his left shoulder – a really great design, fish scales in silver and black, that makes me think of a royal cape thrown over his back – but I notice he isn't wearing his shoes, which is against regulations.

Brian is still hammering away at nothing. He's taller than the other guy; he's got the advantage in height and reach, but I can see he's also lighter. His shoulders are bony and knobbly, with bunched muscles – coat-hanger shoulders. Maybe that's why he puts so much care into drawing uniforms; he's got all the details at his fingertips, all the insignia, the ranks, the colours. I remember high collars, bright blue, and gold and silver braiding, shiny buttons. And he's an expert on weapons as well, they're accurate down to the smallest detail: sometimes you can even read the date of manufacture on a rifle butt. His favourite is the Snider-Enfield MK III carbine, you'd swear he'd camped out with one, dismantled it, oiled it, reassembled it, licked it. He's fascinated by the Maori wars of the 1860s, they're actually his real life, even though he seems to be here with us. You can tell he'd have liked to be the great chief Te Kooti, leader of the resistance and the guerrilla forces. But the thing I've noticed is that he doesn't draw the Maori nearly as accurately as he does the British and their weapons. No, the rebels are always more attractive than in real life, as if they're in a Walt Disney film that glorifies them, and besides they're brandishing shiny tomahawks. Or else they leap out of the bush, their superb skin beaded with dewdrops. But to me that's overdoing it. His Te Kooti is a stunner, armed to the teeth, with a great black beard, a red shirt and knee boots. Te Kooti is a cross between the English officers and the half-naked Maori, he's the man of the future, in a way.

I wonder why the guy Brian is going to fight – that's a big word, I know, for three little practice rounds – doesn't have his shoes. I wonder as well if he's seen Brian's comics. Does he know that Brian draws the Maori rebels with bare feet, while the British wear heavy boots that they crush their victims with? Not to mention their firepower, a hundred times greater, their dogs and the *kupapa* who help them against the insurgents. The trainer ought to ask him to put his sneakers on, but he's in a bad mood after his discussion and he doesn't notice anything when he comes over. It's Brian who stops and points his glove towards the bare feet, while the Maori/Samoan shrugs and shouts something through his mouth-guard, which is no use at all because Ramon isn't listening; he looks at his stopwatch and gives the signal.

Brian might be a Pakeha, but he sides with the Maori, not his own white ancestors that he calls maggots in his comic – which doesn't stop him from fighting, of course, and enjoying it.

Except he's off to a bit of a bad start, throwing stiff, clumsy jabs — it looks as though he's swallowed a bayonet — and he can't keep his opponent at arm's length. The Maori isn't fooling around: he's using the old one-two, one-two, just like on the videos Ramon is always trying to sell us, and Brian has watched them and so he ought to know how to deal with it. Instead, he backs away and gets a pummelling in the chest. He only just dodges the upper-cut that would have ended the match instantly.

Suddenly it hurts me. I want to shout to Brian: 'Stamp on his feet, that'll teach him to break the rules and it'll give you an advantage.' But there's too much going on in a statement like that, what with the idea that the rebels didn't respect the laws and treaties. No, that would put him in the position of the British officers he's so critical of. So I hold my tongue, now and for ever: I feel the sweat cooling on my back and my left hand is suddenly painfully clenched around something – now I know it's not just the taping that's a problem.

The trainer heaves a sigh and spits on the floor. He separates them and asks the Pakeha why he doesn't follow through after the jabs. 'You're staying too high,' he says, 'don't let him get in close like that.' And to the other guy: 'That's good, just don't let your guard down on the right because you think you've got it won.'

In his comics, Brian is really good at insulting the Maori. It's crazy how violent the terms are that he makes the soldiers use. But in fact these racist insults are reserved for the Maori who are helping the soldiers fight Te Kooti, for the *kupapa*, Maori loyal to the Crown, who get called 'big mouthed baboons', 'heathen scumbags', not to mention a few even uglier names I don't want to repeat because we've heard more than enough of that kind of thing in France. Some of these insults do seem to me to have come into use well after the Maori wars.

Back on track after the trainer's advice, Brian throws himself into it with renewed energy. His left is much more effective now, but he still can't get the right to follow through. His opponent isn't outstanding, and he could nail him if he would just keep at it. If he would just . . . To do it, he'd have to blow a circuit in his brain, you can tell, he'd have to clear his mind of Te Kooti and his *toa* – the handsome, half-naked Maori warriors – and drape a uniform over his own shoulders, they're crying out for it. He mustn't let himself be mesmerised by the tattoos glinting on his opponent's left shoulder, he'll have to tell himself something like, he's up against a fake, a Pakeha trying to pass for Maori by getting his back tattooed with a royal cape. That would save him. Instead, he takes a smack on the cheekbone and the trainer has to stop the fight again for a bit. No blood, but he's going to have a terrific bruise. You OK? he asks Brian. You OK? Everyone knows that Brian is a tough customer, he's not going to let himself start imagining that his great-grandfather raped this guy's great-grandmother during one of the Urewera campaigns. No, that kind of idea would stuff him up completely, and it would prove that Ramon is right, always saying,

'If you lose, it's because you deserve to.' Think about something else, Brian!

He's stuffed.

He's a hard man, though, knows the bush better than anyone. He spends half his life there, catching kiwi that he hands over to the biologists working to preserve the species. These valiant scientists tag them and fit them with electronic transmitters so they can get a population count, find out where their burrows are, keep an eye on them and make good citizens of them. It's a lonely job, and it leaves Brian plenty of time to dwell on things. He stays in the bush for days on end, in the rain and the cold, tramping along with his tent on his back and his Winchester slung over one shoulder, on the lookout for the birds, keeping a sharp eye on the undergrowth and the trees, getting his feet wet and scraping the skin off his hands while up above the tui mock him. And he waits for the moon to rise, too, because that's the best time to sing. And boy, does he know how to sing: he imitates the call of the male kiwi and the female comes running. Sometimes it's the other way around, but he's better at the male call. Unequalled. Poised with his knees flexed, ready to pounce, he calls softly, a call that touches the heart of Mrs Kiwi, and she comes running, all excited. Then he pounces. The bird may be quick, but Brian's a rocket, and he's got great stamina, too. Just as the kiwi thrusts her head into her burrow, Brian dives to the ground behind her and grabs her legs, oblivious to her big sharp claws. He pulls her out of her nest. She can struggle all she likes now. Once he got his wrist slashed, but he was so triumphant that he didn't feel the pain and didn't let go. He licked away the blood. That's the way it is in wartime – but not in the ring, where he's just taken three blows that have knocked the wind out of him so badly that he's gasping for air, and it burns his throat as he breathes in. He waves his arms around like a windmill, but it's not much use.

He had a photo taken of himself holding a female kiwi with one hand, his fist clamped around her legs. He got his wife to take the photo when she went on one of his trips and spent the whole time complaining that her magazine was limp because of the dampness at night. But they did make out on the grass, and as he thrust into her Brian was thinking, Oh yes, she likes that, the bitch.

To get himself excited. And boy, does he ever know how to get himself excited.

But not out loud, because he really wants her to be quiet. Not a single word, not a single moan, so he can keep his mind clear and stay as stiff as a bayonet.

He's crazy about uniforms and he's jealous of his wife when she comes.

If only he could imagine something else, he wouldn't be taking a pasting this evening. He's beaten himself up. He hates soldiers and loves their uniforms – soldiers who kill the handsome young barefoot Maori.

When the trainer stops the bout, he says sharply to Brian, 'You didn't even fight.'

★

My left fist still won't open, as if it's holding on to stolen money. Banknotes that I wouldn't want to show anyone. And even under the shower my fist doesn't relax: maybe I've strained a ligament. When I go out into the parking area, I'm happy to see David waiting for me, but in fact the reason he's there is because he's deep in discussion with a bloke who's as wide as he is tall, a bloke with spectacular muscles straining his singlet.

I know him too, I've seen him in the weights room pumping iron. Lying on his back, crushed beneath the bar he was trying to lift, his face purple, his eyes practically popping out of their sockets, and the veins on his forehead looking like a map of the Alps. He looked to me as if he'd been made up for a horror movie. But now here he is outside in the fading light, shiny as a celluloid doll, and I'm relieved to see he'll be with us for a while yet. David doesn't introduce me and we get into his car.

Exhaustion hits me as the engine starts to purr. I'd like to go for a drive around the harbour, but David has only one thing on his mind, and he's unswerving.

'That guy,' he says carefully after a minute, 'that guy in the parking area, I can have the same muscles as him in four months. He said, "Why stay a skinny runt when we can fix that for you for a few measly bucks?"'

'A skinny runt?'

Anabolic steroids, testosterone and all the rest, he'll be buying them tomorrow.

I reckon it's dangerous, he's risking his life playing

around with syringes. 'If I'd known, I'd have let you beat me.'

He shakes his head. So here's one more guy determined not to be himself. When I say this he looks at me as though my English is even more incomprehensible than usual. And growls, 'Myself? Being myself is having muscles. Real muscles like in magazine photos.'

These are the times we live in, cosmetic surgery and organ replacements: you go for it, whether the lights are red or not, you transform yourself. We're just DNA, after all.

I was cradling my left arm against my chest and it felt as if my hand was swollen. That's what I'd got for thrashing David. A minute later we were driving along beside the harbour, obviously, because we were on the way home from the Hutt, and I smiled as I imagined that David's route and mine were finally coming together – yet another illusion, because we'd never taken mine. In front of us the lights of Wellington glittered, shining redly in the night, proudly braced against an emptiness they'd never be able to encircle. And then on the left, on the horizon, an inexplicable band of pale light.

That's where we come from, I was sure of it, because there was light and there was you, the girl I'd left behind me. I tried to find the words that would heal our wounds, our bodies stunned by so many blows, the words I most wanted to hear. First I thought of 'I love you', but I knew that by themselves those words could be threatening, that more than once they'd floated around us as we lay there in the darkness, trying to attach themselves, to stab us like needles. What I liked most, when morning came, was the moment when you looked through the window at the clear blue sky, with a little wisp of cloud caught on the crossbar of the window frame. And you said, 'Summer's here for us too.' Yes, for us, and free of charge – you always looked for the catch in anything free.

My arm touching your body, cloud touching cloud, and we laughed with our mouths full of feathers – kiwi, kiwi! Tell me my name, tell me slowly like playing out a ribbon, tell me what my name is.

And my left fist begins to open.

NIGHT SHIFT

It had been a rough night, full of noise from the house next door, where the students were throwing their Friday-night party – music, shouting, laughing, then, much later, voices in the street, long amorous conversations just in front of my window, and the wooden gate into the garden being shaken as though someone couldn't get it open. I'd been woken several times from bad dreams – one in particular where I was sliding down a steep alley covered in a thin layer of ice; with my stupid leather soles slipping about like cakes of soap, I was skidding away towards one of my friends down below. I told myself she was going to catch me in her arms, of course, but she didn't, she didn't seem to be aware of what was happening to me, just kept on talking about something else, and then, by some miracle, instead of falling flat on my face I managed to make a turn halfway down and stop, like practising a skiing technique. At that point I'd woken up to the sound of footsteps outside, something hitting the fence, and I'd had the impression the students were in the yard, trying the back door, with much swearing and muffled laughter.

In the morning, everything was an unreal blue, calm and serene, even the birds in the cabbage tree were going quietly about their business. Not a single sound from the house next door: the party people seemed to have been wiped out by the return of daylight, I pictured them lying tousled in their rumpled sheets, arms outstretched across greasy couches between mounds of empty beer bottles, watched over by the red eyes of stereos endlessly waiting to be fed a CD.

In this stunning, almost suspicious silence, I slipped outside and when I got to St David Street I saw that the wind had brought down masses and masses of leaves during the night: a huge multicoloured carpet, green, brown, red and yellow, covering the asphalt, the footpaths and the field where just yesterday the students had been playing rugby. What now stretched in front of me was a park lined with majestic trees all the way to the university, all the way to the Leith, all the way to the harbour. My feet walked on unfamiliar soil, the sound of my footsteps was muffled, and I cleared my throat as if I was afraid I might discover my voice had changed as well while I was asleep.

And the sun I'd thought would be gone for days had come back in the wake of the storm. It was shining so brightly! Instead of going to the library as I'd intended, I decided to stop at the Green Acorn and have a coffee at one of the two metal tables outside. Sitting by myself in the sun with russet leaves all around me, I felt a little as though I'd landed on this flying carpet under my feet – and I felt good, even more incognito than usual. The young waitress who brought me my short black was wearing a tight-fitting T-shirt, her breasts stretching the black fabric and its big white letters out of shape: J-U-N-G-L-E C-A-F-E, and when I raised my eyes to meet hers I didn't dare inquire what café, what jungle – something underneath the letters, maybe? I just asked instead what the big trees around us were called, because the leaves must have come from them, even if they showed no sign of it, their huge branches innocently swaying, so densely covered with leaves that you would have sworn they had lost none at all. But the waitress shrugged her shoulders, the letters of J-U-N-G-L-E shifted, and she couldn't tell me what they were called. 'I see them every day,' she said, 'but I don't call them anything.'

I stayed out in the sunshine that was warming everything; for once, the blue and white-striped umbrella set up on the footpath seemed to have a purpose, as did the lush plants in their pots and the insect slowly climbing up the wall, following the outline of the shadow of my head and slipping through the black fingers cast by the fern. Yes, suddenly everything was in its place, perfect, better than anyone could have arranged it, but how could I hold on to that moment, stop it from slipping into the next one and disappearing? We could have been anywhere, in a painting by Matisse, for example, or Frances Hodgkins, who grew up here. The summer that had slunk away in shame was back in force, shining out on all sides, from the ground, the walls, the plants, the table where I'd put down my cup, my body, and the leaves beneath my feet. It brought a happiness that pulled the sky and the earth closer together, a kind of natural libido that demanded nothing of us, just gave, gave and gave again, blissfully rising above the sad little lives of us two-legged creatures.

It was later, with Will in his rattly old Toyota, that I became aware of the other side of the dead leaves. Of course, Will had no idea what the JUNGLE CAFE was. Just some commercial brand-name, he said, or else a cryptic code name for Jesus Christ . . . And we left it at that. I have to say we had our minds on other things. We were on the long road down Signal Hill, because Will had wanted to stop off at his place to get a book about the infestations of didymo and other deadly organisms threatening the island's ecosystem.

Will Somerville is the only real genius I've ever had anything to do with. He could read all the European languages and spoke five or six of them perfectly. When I first met him, I asked him how long ago he'd left France to live in Dunedin, and he smiled indulgently. Because in fact he'd come from London, and the only reason he'd come back to Dunedin, where he had studied, was to live with a woman from here that he'd met in England. Not long after they moved, the woman went off to Auckland, and now he was on his own in a house lent to him by a couple who were living overseas. And that was where he worked from home for a translation company based in Hamburg, in Germany. They sent him business letters, contracts and other documents to translate into English. They were usually urgent orders that Tranzlingua (with the 'z' in italics) e-mailed him in the evenings (mornings, for Will) and received when the office opened in the morning. In this way Tranzlingua was able to guarantee speedy service for its time-pressured clients, charging top rates for the work on the grounds that it was night-shift work. In the beginning, Will found this system beneficial because it gave him a certain degree of security: Tranzlingua couldn't easily replace him with a translator in Germany or the rest of Europe, who would in fact need to be paid at night rates. But two years into it, he was tired of seeing the whole day taken up by this solitary activity. 'I'm always somewhere else,' he said, 'in some other language, off in my cyber-nowhere.'

Not in Europe, not here.

He'd become invisible.

I just wondered how a man with such a brain could be satisfied with this kind of life.

I believe we met because we both felt like strangers – not just here, but everywhere. I'd come to Dunedin on a research trip, I hung out in libraries mostly, and Will had introduced me to Bill Manhire's famous line: 'I live at the edge of the universe'. He didn't leave out the start of the following line either: 'like everybody else', which made us so ordinary and even more lonely.

Since his partner had left him, the person he

talked to most regularly was Kirsten, the secretary at Tranzlingua. A friendly note on his screen every morning. Sometimes a few minutes on the phone. He kept in touch at weekends as well. She sent him photos of herself and her daughter. He'd been in on all the details of her divorce.

'She may come here on holiday,' he said. The next minute he wondered whether he shouldn't go and join her in Europe. Letting her come to New Zealand, that was . . .

Lost in thought, he eased off the accelerator, laying his forearm across the steering-wheel as if he was going to stop – a bare, muscular forearm. Will didn't seem to notice the cold; he was in his forties, quite athletic.

Suddenly he turned right, under the trees, down a narrow roadway covered in dead leaves. You could see the tracks of vehicles that had passed recently, crushing the leaves and stripping the asphalt bare. A pretty road that was turning more and more into a forest track, where I could sometimes see water running alongside it. 'A shortcut,' Will said, adding, 'This would be perfect for a four-wheel-drive.'

He was right, the road was really steep and winding. The car was slipping on the curves – you could hear the wheels spinning for a second or two as the motor roared and mud or wet leaves sprayed up against the undercarriage – then taking off with a jerk.

Will kept on talking, still calm, although he was gripping the steering-wheel with both hands and I could see a blue vein pulsing on his forearm. His voice was even, almost monotonous, as steady as the sound of the motor. But the more the car skidded, the more we talked about preposterous things. I quoted the *Guinness Book of Records* where I'd read that someone had eaten his entire bike, including the handlebars, tyres and racing gears. There'd even been a record-holder who, over a period of two years, swallowed a whole plane – just a two-seater, admittedly, but still a plane. Will, who had managed to bring in the Rotenburg cannibal (he'd followed the trial on the Internet during the nights when he couldn't sleep), was shaking his head and saying there were some things all the same that were inedible, and quoted the anecdote about the death of Josef Mengele that he'd read in the *Guardian*. The former Nazi butcher was so worried he'd be caught in his hiding-place in South America that he used to chew the ends of his moustache, from nerves. So he swallowed bits of hair that he apparently couldn't digest: they built up into a ball that blocked his intestine.

Will was now speaking in jerky sentences; more precisely, he was punctuating them by hitting the brake. I could feel my own toes clenching, scratching at the insides of my shoes as if they were trying to break out. It's a bit of a habit of mine to work at my insoles this way, but here on this dangerous descent it was turning into a second conversation: my feet were saying something quite different from my tongue, and they were forcing me to listen. My toes were searching for solid land. They were trying to go right through the shoes and the floor, to brake and stop the Toyota, prevent it from smashing into a house or a tree.

And then, while Will was still going on about the 'hairball' that had killed Mengele – very similar, he said, to the ones owls bring back up – the car surged to the top of a steep path covered with such a beautiful carpet of dead leaves that I wouldn't have been surprised to see a bunch of kids hurtling down it on sleds. 'Stop!' I shouted. But the Toyota had already taken off. Veering to the left, it charged over what must normally have been a footpath and headed onto a lawn, where it spun around, swinging halfway back onto the roadway before coming to a standstill, almost gracefully, the two front wheels wedged in a hole.

We were thrown forward, stopped by our seat-belts. I rubbed my hand slowly across my forehead, to feel myself: this was all too similar to my dream of the previous night. The engine was still running. 'Fucking leaves,' whispered Will.

We got out. Will knelt down beside the wheels. The tread in the tyres was covered over by a sticky paste, a mixture of mud and leaves that he tried to pry off with his nails. A complete waste of time. He stood up, looked around. We were in front of a house, but no one seemed to have seen or heard us. 'Let's leave the car,' Will said, 'I'll call a towtruck, we're not far from my place.'

We set off on foot without saying another word about the shortcut. It was still a fine day, the sky still had that innocent, blue look about it, my feet were relaxing, and even if I wasn't wearing the most suitable shoes – in this situation, Will's big greyish trainers, probably Nike Airs, were better than my dainty footwear, like cyclists' shoes, all soft shiny leather – I was pleased to feel the spongy ground beneath my feet.

I said, 'You can't overestimate the importance of shoes for the morale.'

I left it at that, didn't tell Will what my first grown-up shoes had meant to me. The first pair that showed I wasn't satisfied any more with just looking vaguely fashionable, I could also make an investment, assert my identity, want my feet to be more comfortable. This desire had been there all along, only emerging the day I was struck by the sight of the shoes worn by a man in front of me buying a newspaper. They were a revelation. I was blind to everything but those shoes: their shiny metal D-rings (later I would learn there were twelve of them), their wide, flat laces zigzagging up to the ankles, the sides marked with three stitched scars – oh, those unmistakable lines that transformed the so-pale toes nestling inside. Mephisto shoes! That name had such power, such mana, and I quickly found practical reasons to justify my choice: the suppleness of the hard-wearing soles, the Gore-Tex lining and the heel padding, arch support, air-circulatory insoles, Norwegian stitching . . . I bought them, they were mine, and with their help I was going to find a foothold in life, I could keep pace with anyone, in the city or the country, come summer, come winter, in restaurants, in the car, wherever I went. And they would never go out of style either, they were beyond style. They would be faithful companions I could depend on for the rest of my life. I would have sworn that, back then; but in fact I hadn't worn Mephistos for quite a while. How had I moved away from them? Suddenly I saw why, right at that moment, so long afterwards, trekking through this Dunedin suburb: they'd disappeared with the woman I'd been in love with. Once she was gone, my Mephistos had changed, they'd become heavy, complicated, dowdy, good for every occasion and therefore good for none. They pretty much fell off my feet, so to speak. Instead, I'd gone back to having a different pair for everything, for evening and morning, for sailing and walking, sandals, sneakers, boots – a whole cupboard full. I'd even bought a shoe organiser, thinking it would be a rational solution to my mess, but as soon as I'd brought it into my little apartment it turned out to be ugly, badly designed and just another addition to the clutter.

It was during this surfeit of footwear that I became aware how much my feet kept digging away at the insoles of my shoes. So I bought inserts to slip in, made of polar fleece, latex, leather, with activated carbon, shock-absorbing, deodorising – it didn't really matter what they were made of, my toes burrowed into them, shredded them in no time at all, just like talons or claws. I'd started to inspect my tracks on the sand as well, at the beach, where I noticed that the front part of my foot went in deep, whereas the heel hardly left a mark – but what should I make of this observation?

'What do you think of mine?' Will called.

We were now walking up a clean, open street, one of the ones we should have driven along in the Toyota.

'Yours? Lift up your foot.'

He was still tracking clumps of leaves stuck to his soles. Probably he could hardly feel the ground beneath his feet. And his big trainers had lost their colour: they were greyish, battered, bloated, they made his feet look like babies wrapped in blankets. Suffering.

I told him they were crying for their mummy.

We arrived at his house, a long narrow building on the side of the hill, half-hidden by shrubs. The garage driveway, covered in leaves, hadn't been swept. As soon as we went inside, I was struck by a feeling of cold and damp, as though the house wasn't really lived in. Will explained that the owners had left their furniture, their books, their pots and pans, their wardrobes stuffed full of clothes, so he'd taken refuge in one bedroom and a little study where he'd set up his two computers. But he'd also covered the windows of the study with newspaper. It was strange. 'I was thinking about setting it up as a dark room,' he said, 'and then I found it was really quite comfortable.' He had probably wanted to shut himself away, because he'd stuck up pages of newsprint between the windows as well; the wall on the garden side of the room was completely covered by them. The light from outside filtered through the yellowed paper with its lines of black letters. As I went closer, I noticed that these weren't the kind of newspapers that you find in your mailbox and that often get used for chores around the house. Apart from one *Otago Daily Times* and a *New Zealand Herald*, most of them weren't even in English: there were *Svenska Dagbladet, Basler Zeitung, Die Zeit, Le Monde,* Polish and Russian papers – the languages Will translated, the ones he lived in.

'Reams of papers,' I said.

He thought I'd said 'dreams', and said yes, it was a sort of dream.

In any case, it was unreal, and I thought I understood why Will claimed he never felt the cold.

First he turned on a little lamp on a low table, which gave off a feeble yellow light, then the computer. After clearing the top of an ottoman so I could sit down, he stayed on his feet, rolling a joint to help us forget about the incident in the car.

I took a few drags, looking at the long strips of yellowed papers on the walls. While I was doing this Will printed out some information about an algae even more destructive than didymo, something called *Undaria pinnatifida.* He held out an official pamphlet that described it as 'a stowaway illegally introduced into the ballast waters of foreign ships'.

An immigrant devouring the country's coasts.

'Couldn't it have come from a New Zealand ship?' I asked. 'Is that really out of the question?'

The joint was making me want to laugh.

At that point a photo of Kirsten popped up on the screen. We both looked at it for a moment. I couldn't have said much about it, except that she was smiling, but her face was a bit distorted by being enlarged. The photo, the pixels, the screen, everything was bothering me and I started blinking.

Will turned towards me, a sheet of paper in his hand: Kirsten's last message sent that same morning, a dream her eight-year-old daughter had had, which Kirsten thought was very funny. He read it out, translating as he went: it was the story of a guy who talked nonsense; in fact, he was repeating the words of the frog on top of his head, and people took him seriously without ever noticing the frog.

I didn't find this dream especially funny, but Will laughed as he read it out, just as proud as if it had come from his own daughter. And then at the end of the message Kirsten asked: do you think it could have anything to do with the divorce?

We were both pretty puzzled. How could a dream like that have any connection with the kid's parents' divorce?

Who could say? Not me, nor did I want to ask Will why Kirsten was showing off her daughter in an attempt to seduce him. I was getting pretty high by now, my feet were relaxing, and I felt comfortable enough to tell Will he should deal with this damn wall of papers, this dead, blind landscape, before Kirsten got here. Yes, of course, he agreed, he completely understood what was wrong: he'd pull it all down and finally look out at the garden, the trees, the roof of the house next door, life in this place, the whole works. But he came back almost straight away to his questions, his doubts; wouldn't it be better if he went to Europe to join Kirsten?

'And got some new shoes,' I said. 'That's essential, it's just not happening with those ones.'

We were quiet for a moment.

Now that I could see the situation so very clearly, I suggested he should take my shoes. Our feet were pretty much the same size. They were a seducer's shoes, mine were, they had proven themselves, they would make him feel confident.

'I'm giving them to you,' I said.

He was flabbergasted. I watched his blue eyes floating behind his glasses, his gaze wandering from my feet to the newspapers blocking the windows, then from nothing in particular to nothing in particular, his mind working overtime until, suddenly reaching a decision, he shook his head and said:

'No, no, I can't take yours. You're on your own.'

PAEKAKARIKI

You would tell me, 'It's time.'
Then you'd go away and I'd get up.

The strange thing is that your words come back to me
today, lying here on the beach, my left ear filled with
the low sighing of the waves collapsing on the sand and
my right buzzing with the cicadas' shrill chorus. Maybe
it's this racket that allows your words to surface.

Steven and the others didn't want to stay out in the
sun, so they'd gone for a walk along the water's edge,
past the driftwood on the high-tide line, between the
twisted dead grey branches swept out to sea by the rivers,
carried on the tides, finally abandoned here. Couldn't we
use them to build a big fire and roast a sheep? We would
dedicate the fat and the smoke to the gods, according to
custom, and when the juice ran down our fingers we'd
wipe them on the sand or on our bodies.

You wouldn't approve. You'd just shake your head
and I'd know.

What I remember most is the sound of your voice; of your face I can recall only a certain sadness, and perhaps a trace of something morbid. There was a snideness, a subtle poison, in people's compliments when they said you looked like Humphrey Bogart.

When I open my eyes again I notice something is different: the colours have started to bleed. I see it first in the sky, where the blue has torn itself away from the white, trailing streaks across the outlines, then in the leaves with their green smudged over the edges like a careless painting, and even further away on the flag where the orange and yellow have drifted outside the margins. I tell myself that all this must be because of the glare, I try blinking, but nothing goes back to its proper place. That's the sort of day it is, I've known times where even words couldn't come close to what they were supposed to mean, where I took comfort in the thought that at least my shadow was hard on my heels. And through all these gaps there's a white, unreal light spreading across the sand and the water. It shines down on a bird just in front of me, a black one, not much bigger than a blackbird or a tui. He's full of confidence, attacking a piece of rotten wood with his beak. As the splinters fly he pulls out worms or insects and swallows them, lifting his head towards the sky, then starting to peck again. A fearless bird that doesn't even let the gulls put him off when they try to settle right beside him with a great flapping of wings.

Hammer away, I tell him, hammer away! As if he were avenging some old grievance of mine. His beak is so strong, so precise: Katherine Mansfield's pen must have been just like that. He gives me so much pleasure, to me he's a perfect machine, one of my dreams come to life. Every rap of his beak announces it proudly: summer has come to Paekakariki, and all our sins are forgiven!

And yet I'm the one who frightened this wonderful bird away, sitting up because there was a long line, a whole army of children approaching from the far end of the beach. They looked like bees in their brown-and-orange-striped shirts, with their hats sitting roundly on their heads. They stamped their little feet on the hard sand and held their arms close in to their chests like folded wings, buzzing as they came, 'Fit, fit, fittest.' They went past very close, not looking at me, in a long procession back to the slowpokes, the very last ones, the lost ones. The out-of-breath little girl who sighed through a bubble of spit, 'We're training . . . we're getting fit.'

After they'd gone I felt lonely and decided to go to the café to look for the people who'd brought me here in their car. The colours still weren't properly inside their outlines, but I wasn't going to let that bother me any more, no, I was going to pretend today was just another of those ordinary days whose only merit is that they eventually end.

In the café we hid it all away behind laughter and jokes, and I remember feeling a bit envious of the green parrot painted on the wall because it could simply be there without having to say a thing.

We were drinking wine in spite of the heat. By the third glass, the bubbles had started to sing and Tony suggested the shops and cafés in the street should be knocked flat, including the wall with the painted green parrot, and rebuilt further down beside the sea. Put a bulldozer through the lot and start again from scratch. It would be good for business, he said, and we'd be sitting there looking at the wide blue horizon. We'd see ourselves as if in a mirror, and the surf would sing softly in our hearts . . .

Steven didn't agree, absolutely not; he thought that was the kind of idea some Nazi architect might have had.

Katie had been studying the room for some time. 'I can prove I'm a lesbian,' she said.

Everyone thought everyone else was a riot.

The shadows were lengthening like knives and we shouldn't have stayed in our bare feet. Lizzie told us the few acres of land the Wakefield Company allocated to one of her ancestors were so steep that a horse couldn't stay upright on the slope. She looked at the railway line. 'No trains in those days, either.' Her ancestor, she went on, had given everything he had to buy this land that he thought was flat – he'd even gone into debt – only to find himself faced with such a sharp incline he had to climb it on his hands and knees, like a goat.

'He didn't commit suicide?' I asked.

'I'm here, aren't I?' she answered.

As if that proved anything. I'm here too. But her reply had silenced me. The wine in my glass started to swirl, and I told myself that you were here as well. This was the second time today I'd felt your presence, and I still didn't understand why. Usually you were far away, or rather you were so deeply ingrained in me that you'd taken the form of some of my thoughts and gestures, and this made you invisible. But there you were, that afternoon in Paekakariki, probably because of the gap between the colours and the outlines. My soul, when you died, was still a child's – is it ever any different for us, in our father's eyes? The thought that you might be inside my soul filled me with speechless horror; up till now I'd always fought to be alone in my body. Had I lost that fight too?

The only time we'd clashed that I could remember, you'd won hands down by showing me how inhuman my strength was. One Sunday morning on the California freeway, on the way home from church, you were talking to me as you drove along, about your difficult life, about Mom and the divorce, and I rebelled, I said I wasn't the one you should be pouring your heart out to. The car swerved across into another lane, just some crumpled metal and nobody died that time, but it was like a dress rehearsal. Standing there on the hard shoulder you looked a bit distraught, and there I was, stiff as a board on the outside and totally shocked on the inside, wondering how mere words could have had such an impact. My words.

You were the child, and, at fourteen, I was the father trying to stop you from destroying us.

Now I realised that I'd started feeling sick when

Lizzie made that comment about being here. Because in fact I haven't been entirely here for a long time. I believe I've forgotten you, I know I wouldn't be able to describe you, and yet just hearing you breathing on the other end of the phone would be enough for me to know it's you. Or else you turn up in one of my dreams. I'm driving and you're sitting in the back seat wearing your flying jacket. You don't say much – your worried expression is enough to tell me I'm not going in the right direction. Should I make a right turn, or go left? Turn around and go back? I stare into the rear-view mirror, I study the expression in your eyes and try to read there the way ahead. I don't have an accident.

I can't drive all by myself, but my shrink insists that you obviously committed suicide all by yourself. Nothing to do with me or the words I spoke. Nobody could have stopped you, he says.

If only you could really leave me, die properly. That wouldn't be the end of me, would it?

'I'm here, aren't I?' Lizzie repeats with a strange pride, as if my question had offended her.

We're the survivors, and therefore the fittest. The product of hundreds of thousands of years of evolution, that's us. Could there be any greater proof of our worth?

I feel as if we're rising with the wind. In the street some Jesus freak has set up a sign. He calls out 'Jesus loves you', pointing to this love bleeding on a dried-out old wooden cross. His offsider tries to hand us pamphlets, printed in big letters: NO, MAN IS NOT DESCENDED FROM

THE APES. Isn't it strange, this insistence on believing that God wanted him, especially, to be just the way he is? Perhaps his God even speaks to him, as well. Are they born-agains? Steven asks. Are they the ones who believe in the rapture and in Armageddon? They're all going to Heaven in ten years' time, or three. I wish it was straight away, this evening, we're so keen to see them go flying up.

I say 'we', and I feel sad because I know you wouldn't want to see me in such company.

A quarter of an hour in the car and we wind up at Lizzie's place. She wants to show us the two deer that live behind her house, in a pen where they haven't eaten all the shrubs yet. One of the deer is small, light brown, and looks like Bambi; the other is big and dark and lifts his antlered head, anxious. You can see his muscles twitching under his black coat; he makes you want to touch him because you can tell he's poised for flight, and when you do touch him you'll have that delicious feeling of taming something wild. Lizzie passes us some bok choy leaves: if you push them through the holes in the fence and wave them about the deer will come and eat out of your hands, she says.

But when Steven and Katie put their Chinese cabbage through the fence, it's Lizzie's dog that rushes up, a very pale cocker spaniel that's managed to slip into the enclosure: he stands on his hind legs and snatches one of the leaves and chews and swallows it. And Lizzie laughs her head off. The surprise she wanted to show us was her vegetarian cocker spaniel, Snowy. He got so jealous watching everyone making a fuss of the deer, she says, that he started eating what they eat. He's stealing their limelight, and when it comes down to it *they're all just children.* 'Isn't that right, Snowy?' she asks, stroking him as he rolls on his back at her feet. She goes on about the Garden of Eden where no animal ate another, where they must all have been vegetarians. But Katie protests: what makes us think plants don't suffer?

This dog makes me sick. He didn't degrade himself to this extent all on his own. He reminds me of those idiotic, saccharine versions of 'Little Red Riding Hood' where the wolf can't even eat the grandmother any more. Snowy, Lizzie's cocker spaniel, Lizzie's son. Suddenly I feel sorry for him, I hate Lizzie, and then I pull myself together, my disgust seems out of proportion – after all, even if she's flattered that her dog has turned into an occasional vegetarian, jealous of the deer, is she really responsible for this? This unnatural canine, this pseudo-human rolling on his back and eating cabbage, this poor castrated show-off, deprived of meat, sleeping at his mistress's feet or on her bed, maybe even *in* her bed, he's like me, after all. I'd already felt a connection with that black bird early this afternoon. Only human beings seem eternally distant from me. And I wondered if that's because of you. If I could blame you for it.

We set off again. I found myself in a car with people whose names I didn't know, and had that rather pleasant feeling of being nowhere, always between two places, when we pulled up at the house of the artist with blue hair. Actually, she'd woven lengths of neon blue wool into her dyed black hair, and her house, huge and glowing in the light of the setting sun, stood in the middle of an artificial-looking garden. Walking down the mosaic-decorated pathways edged with big blue flowers, passing the stone benches where statues covered in ceramic fragments were baking in the sun – they were couples, sometimes grotesque with their wings and crowns, but mostly, touchingly naive – it was as if I were moving towards the edge of the world. Or rather it was in the big sitting room flooded with light, in front of the fireplace with its solid totara surround, between the imposing animal-shaped sculptures and the absurd machines that reminded me of Tinguely's, that I began to feel that the world was ending. The feeling came from the music playing very softly, apparently night and day, a never-ending music with a rhythm as repetitive as the cicadas', the best-known tunes of last century in a monotonous arrangement making the original melodies so bland that, although they were recognisable, you could really only hear them from memory, and the world in turn was no more substantial than nostalgia. From this point on, everything would be smooth and muffled, as if buried under a very gentle snowfall that would deaden our voices and our footsteps.

That's when I heard you say it again.

It's time.

In the past, when you said these words you'd be standing behind my bedroom door, telling me it was time to get up and go to school. I could probably hear the resignation in your voice, because after you'd gone these words always seemed to me to be your way of preparing for death. Of letting yourself be weighed down, day after day.

But in the house of the blue-haired artist, what was this 'time'? Time to leave, time to stay? To follow you, or to go out into the world? Your time, mine? Were we still tied together by these words, like a piece of rope with each of us holding on to one end? I stood there for a moment, perplexed, lost among all these objects that had no proper name any more, and then my own voice, unexpectedly, very clear:

'I don't know you.'

WHERE WE LIVE

Standing on his balcony on the opposite side of the street, he took a drag on his cigarette, enjoying the cool evening air. His wife, wearing a red dress, looked a bit Asian to me, at least as far as I could tell from fifteen metres away. She was watering the last of the plants. He was paying no attention to her, or to what was going on behind him. He was standing next to the wrought-iron railing, wearing a white singlet and flexing his muscles, making the blueish tattoo on his biceps dance.

I'm always envious of how calm he seems, this man in the house across the street. He's just there because he has the right to be there, because he wants to. He's there because he pays his rent, he smokes his fags and flexes his muscles. I imagine what he's thinking – for example, about the American movie he's just watched on TV. It's the story of a guy like him, a hard man you don't want to cross. But someone does cross him, he strikes back, he's even badder than the bad guys, he gets everything sorted, and now he's chilling out on his balcony, smoking, and the water's running off the geraniums down onto the pedestrians on Rue Tiquetonne.

And now our defender of law and order is being forced to take action again. I can sense that he's reluctant, I can almost hear him sighing that you never get any peace and quiet around here, that it's always up to him. He starts shouting angrily, in a deep voice, a smoker's rasp. Louder and louder. In the end he's bawling it out, attacking the people who live on the second floor, but on our side of the street, in *our* house.

'If I have to come over there, I'll show you how to screw! Can't you pull your bloody blinds down?'

There's a couple of junkies on the second floor. I can tell what they're up to from the tattooed man's indignation. The junkies are young, they've got a filthy old mattress, a few clothes piled up on chairs, and they're going at it under the bright light of the naked bulb dangling from the ceiling, not bothering to shoo away the flies or close the shutters. The tattooed guy across the street can say what he likes, they're not about to stop. He should leave them alone, for God's sake, or congratulate them, even. Does he think it's easy, making love when you're doped to the eyeballs? Actually, it's a bit of an achievement.

But Mr Tattoo isn't about to stop. 'If I have to come over there, I'll give you something else to think about, I'll cut it right off . . .'

His wife puts her hand on his shoulder: 'Calm down, Raymond.'

He shoves her hand away, and his wife, still holding the watering can, sprays Raymond's trousers.

'Watch what you're doing!' he shouts, furious.

'Oh, do shut up,' she says.

And there they go, having a row on the sixth floor. The passers-by don't look up; the street's too narrow for them to be able to see the show, but from the second floor, from the lovers' greasy bed comes a response: 'Keep it down up there, can't you? You're putting me off.'

Things are turning nasty up on the sixth floor: the woman's shouting that he should just try it and see, try it and see where it gets him.

She's beautiful in her red dress. She's just sunk her sharp nails into his arm. He says, 'A-a-a-h, you bitch!' The flood of insults is punctuated by blows. They fall into the flowers, twisting about in a tangle, the live cigarette fell into the street long ago, bye-bye peaceful evening. The guy on the second floor, totally defeated, leans sadly out of his window. 'The bastards . . . Charlie, we were almost there,' says the woman beside him. There's a melancholy tone to her voice.

I keep back a bit, standing in the bay of my fourth-floor window. In the flat to my left, I know Blomet will be watching the performance too. I can hear him but I can't see him, although I'm picturing him in my mind's eye, his enormous belly bulging in his overalls. I hear him shout at his idiot son: 'Don't look, you dope, go and see your mother!' I repeat this sentence to myself, now that there's nothing to watch except the trembling of the crushed leaves on the geraniums – but I'm anticipating what must come next, oh yes, indeed. I say it again to myself: 'Don't look, go and see your mother!'

Big fat Blomet, suddenly happy, starts humming a tune into the night air. Down below, innocent passers-by carry on passing by, of course; and where are they off to anyway, if not to the Fountain of the Innocents? I'm still waiting for the finale, the closing scene, when Aurélie suddenly appears beside me. She was going to put her hand on my shoulder but doesn't, and instead she just says, not without a certain derision, 'So this is the human race you put so much faith in?'

And I reply: 'Have you got an alternative version to offer, then? Have you got another version?'

Predictably, she shrugs her shoulders. She's got plenty of other versions. You just have to choose the one you prefer, she thinks. In fact, this faith is the reason why she has plans for the future, a career. Whereas when I envisage a career, all I can see is a French window opening in front of me (in the house opposite once again, I almost think of it as home). It reveals a huge plant, really lush, a philodendron or similar. More importantly, in front of the plant, on the balcony of this obviously eighteenth-century building, who should appear but Snow White, with her black hair and her lips made even redder by the dying rays of the sun. Snow White has a job in the movie business. Her sister told me this, one afternoon when she was out on the balcony. We were having a conversation across the street, up above the world. Her sister – or maybe her step-sister – has blond hair like Rapunzel, and because I call her Rapunzel I don't remember her real name any more. With Rapunzel I could fancy myself as Prince Charming, but with Snow White I'm just the eighth dwarf, the one nobody knows.

Snow White glances warily at big fat Blomet, lets her gaze linger a bit on the junkie on the second floor who still can't get it up and hasn't stopped shouting insults at the tattooed guy on the sixth floor: 'I hope you're proud of yourself now, you old bastard, you piece of old army surplus . . .' and other such enlightened remarks.

'Are you going to stand there gawking for much longer?' Aurélie asks me.

'No, the show's over. I've got my characters. There's the tattooed guy and his wife, the junkies on the second floor, Blomet and his moron of a son, Rapunzel, Snow White . . .'

'Quite a line-up!' she says mockingly. 'Are you happy with it, at least? Are you happy with it?'

I don't speak. Snow White and I step back from our windows at the same time. Aurélie's question is still nagging at me. I make like I'm deep in thought so as not to answer. It's as if she always knows better than I do how things are going for me. That's why I love her very much, as well as for all the attention she lavishes on me, but she'd rather that didn't stop me from loving her for other reasons.

Later, when we turn out the bedroom light, the noises start. Like moaning, coming down the chimney.

'It's the translator on the fifth floor,' I tell Aurélie. 'This time I'm sure of it.'

We've noticed that the noises occur at unexpected times, in the middle of the afternoon as well as the middle of the night. At first I'd opted for pigeons cooing, Aurélie for lovers ditto, now we don't comment much any more. We just hope it won't keep us awake.

Through the window that opens onto the courtyard, by the light from the night sky, you can still make out the little table with its scattered papers and Aurélie's glasses. The rest of the room is changing shape, I'm sinking deep into another world, I'm going back to the dreams of sleepers who crush their pillows, drooling onto them their hope that tomorrow will bring what they didn't get today.

And I'm back in a book. It starts with a love story and a girl in it called Gaëlle.

ACKNOWLEDGEMENTS

My thanks to Dagmar Rolf, Bernard Cousinier and Marie-Catherine Vacher for their critical insights. And of course to Marie-Claude Lambotte, for her support.

I would also like to thank the Board of the Randell Cottage Writers' Trust and the French Embassy in New Zealand for giving me the opportunity to spend a few months in Wellington. There I was lucky enough to meet Jean Anderson, who has translated these stories with such extraordinary care and sensitivity.